By the Waters of Babylon

BY THE WATERS OF BABYLON

AND OTHER FANTASIES AND PROPHECIES

STEPHEN VINCENT BENÉT

2014

By the Waters of Babylon was first published in 1937, *The Curfew Tolls* in 1935, *The King of the Cats* in 1929, *Doc Mellhorn and the Pearly Gates* in 1938, *The Last of the Legions* in 1937, *The Blood of the Martyrs* in 1936, and *Into Egypt* in 1939. The first collection of these stories under the title *Fantasies and Prophecies* appeared in *Selected Works of Steven Vincent Benét,* vol. 2, Farrar & Rinehart, 1942.

Copyright © 2014 *Hythloday Press*. While the original works in this volume are in the public domain, the distinctive features of this edition may not be reproduced, displayed, modified or distributed without the express prior written permission of the copyright holder.

Contents

By the Waters of Babylon 1

The Curfew Tolls 17

The King of the Cats 38

Doc Mellhorn and the Pearly Gates 56

The Last of the Legions 79

The Blood of the Martyrs 97

Into Egypt 118

By the Waters of Babylon

By the Waters of Babylon
(1937)

The north and the west and the south are good hunting ground, but it is forbidden to go east. It is forbidden to go to any of the Dead Places except to search for metal and then he who touches the metal must be a priest or the son of a priest. Afterwards, both the man and the metal must be purified. These are the rules and the laws; they are well made. It is forbidden to cross the great river and look upon the place that was the Place of the Gods—this is most strictly forbidden. We do not even say its name though we know its name. It is there that spirits live, and demons—it is there that there are the ashes of the Great Burning. These things are forbidden—they have been forbidden since the beginning of time.

My father is a priest; I am the son of a priest. I have been in the Dead Places near us, with my father—at first, I was afraid. When my father went into the house to search for the metal, I stood by the door and my heart felt small and weak. It was a dead man's house, a spirit house. It did not have the smell of man, though there were old bones in a corner. But it is not fitting that a priest's son should show fear. I looked at the bones in the shadow and kept my voice still.

Then my father came out with the metal—good, strong piece. He looked at me with both eyes but I had not run away. He gave me the metal to hold—I took it and did not die. So he knew that I was truly his son and would be a priest in my time. That was when I was very young—nevertheless, my brothers would not have done it, though they are good hunters. After that, they gave me the good piece of meat and the warm corner of the fire. My father watched over me—he was glad that I should be a priest. But when I boasted or wept without a reason, he punished me more strictly than my brothers. That was right.

After a time, I myself was allowed to go into the dead houses and search for metal. So I learned the ways of those houses—and if I saw bones, I was no longer afraid. The bones are light and old—sometimes they will fall into dust if you touch them. But that is a great sin.

I was taught the chants and the spells—I was taught how to stop the running of blood from a wound and many secrets. A priest must know many secrets—that was what my father said.

If the hunters think we do all things by chants and spells, they may believe so—it does not hurt them. I was taught how to read in the old books and how to make the old writings—that was hard and took a long time. My knowledge made me happy—it was like a fire in my heart. Most of all, I liked to hear of the Old Days and the stories of the gods. I asked myself many questions that I could not answer, but it was good to ask them. At night, I would lie awake and listen to the wind—it seemed to me that it was the voice of the gods as they flew through the air.

We are not ignorant like the Forest People—our women spin wool on the wheel, our priests wear a white robe. We do not eat grubs from the trees, we have not forgotten the old writings, although they are hard to understand. Nevertheless, my knowledge and my lack of knowledge burned in me—I wished to know more. When I was a man at last, I came to my father and said, "It is time for me to go on my journey. Give me your leave."

He looked at me for a long time, stroking his beard, and then he said at last, "Yes. It is time." That night, in the house of the priesthood, I asked for and received purification. My body hurt but my spirit was a cool stone. It was my father himself who questioned me about my dreams.

He bade me look into the smoke of the fire and see—I saw and told what I saw. It was what I have always seen—a river, and, beyond it, a great Dead Place and in it the gods walking. I have always thought about that. His eyes were stern when I told him he was no longer my father but a priest. He said, "This is a strong dream."

"It is mine," I said, while the smoke waved and my head felt light. They were singing the Star song in the outer chamber and it was like the buzzing of bees in my head.

He asked me how the gods were dressed and I told him how they were dressed. We know how they were dressed from the book, but I saw them as if they were before me. When I had finished, he threw the sticks three times and studied them as they fell.

"This is a very strong dream," he said." It may eat you up."

"I am not afraid," I said and looked at him with both eyes. My voice sounded thin in my ears but that was because of the smoke.

He touched me on the breast and the forehead. He gave me the bow and the three arrows.

"Take them," he said. "It is forbidden to travel east. It is forbidden to cross the river. It is forbidden to go to the Place of the Gods. All these things are forbidden."

"All these things are forbidden," I said, but it was my voice that spoke and not my spirit. He looked at me again.

"My son," he said. "Once I had young dreams. If your dreams do not eat you up, you may be a great priest. If they eat you, you are still my son. Now go on your journey."

I went fasting, as is the law. My body hurt but not my heart. When the dawn came, I was out of sight of the village. I prayed and purified myself, waiting for a sign. The sign was an eagle. It flew east.

Sometimes signs are sent by bad spirits. I waited again on the flat rock, fasting, taking no food. I was very still—I could feel the sky above me and the earth beneath. I waited till the sun was beginning to sink. Then three deer passed in the valley going east—they did not mind me or see me. There was a white fawn with them—a very great sign.

I followed them, at a distance, waiting for what would happen. My heart was troubled about going east, yet I knew that I must go. My head hummed with my fasting—I did not even see the panther spring upon the white fawn. But, before I knew it, the bow was in my hand. I shouted and the panther lifted his head from the fawn. It is not easy to kill a panther with one arrow but the arrow went through his eye and into his brain. He died as he tried to spring—he rolled over, tearing at the ground. Then I knew I was meant to go east—I knew that was my journey. When the night came, I made my fire and roasted meat.

It is eight suns' journey to the east and a man passes by many Dead Places. The Forest People are afraid of them but I am not. Once I made my fire on the edge of a Dead Place at night and, next morning, in the dead house, I found a good knife, little rusted. That was small to what came afterward but it made my heart feel big. Always when I looked for game, it was in front of my arrow, and twice I passed hunting parties of the Forest People without their knowing. So I knew my magic was strong and my journey clean, in spite of the law.

Toward the setting of the eighth sun, I came to the banks of the great river. It was half-a-day's journey after I had left the god-road—we do not use the god-roads now for they are falling apart into great blocks of stone, and the forest is safer going. A long way off, I had seen the water through trees but the trees were thick. At last, I came out upon an open place at the top of a cliff. There was the great river below, like a giant in the sun. It is very long, very wide. It could eat all the streams we know and still be thirsty. Its name is Ou-dis-sun, the Sacred, the Long. No man of my tribe had seen it, not even my father, the priest. It was magic and I prayed.

Then I raised my eyes and looked south. It was there, the Place of the Gods.

How can I tell what it was like—you do not know. It was there, in the red light, and they were too big to be houses. It was there with the red light upon it, mighty and ruined. I knew that in another moment the gods would see me. I covered my eyes with my hands and crept back into the forest.

Surely, that was enough to do, and live. Surely it was enough to spend the night upon the cliff. The Forest People themselves do not come near. Yet, all through the night, I knew that I should have to cross the river and walk in the places of the gods, although the gods ate me up. My magic did not help me at all and yet there was a fire in my bowels, a fire in my mind. When the sun rose, I thought, "My journey has been clean. Now I will go home from my journey." But, even as I thought so, I knew I could not. If I went to the Place of the Gods, I would surely die, but, if I did not go, I could never be at peace with my spirit again. It is better to lose one's life than one's spirit, if one is a priest and the son of a priest.

Nevertheless, as I made the raft, the tears ran out of my eyes. The Forest People could have killed me without fight, if they had come upon me then, but they did not come.

When the raft was made, I said the sayings for the dead and painted myself for death. My heart was cold as a frog and my knees like water, but the burning in my mind would not let me have peace. As I pushed the raft from the shore, I began my death song—I had the right. It was a fine song.

"I am John, son of John," I sang. "My people are the Hill People. They are the men.
I go into the Dead Places but I am not slain.
I take the metal from the Dead Places but I am not blasted.
I travel upon the god-roads and am not afraid. E-yah! I have killed the panther, I have killed the fawn!
E-yah! I have come to the great river. No man has come there before.
It is forbidden to go east, but I have gone, forbidden to go on the great river, but I am there.
Open your hearts, you spirits, and hear my song.
Now I go to the Place of the Gods, I shall not return.
My body is painted for death and my limbs weak, but my heart is big as I go to the Place of the Gods!"

All the same, when I came to the Place of the Gods, I was afraid, afraid. The current of the great river is very strong—it gripped my raft with its hands. That was magic, for the river itself is wide and calm. I could feel evil spirits about me, I was swept down the stream. Never have I been so much alone—I tried to think of my knowledge, but it was a squirrel's heap of winter nuts. There was no strength in my knowledge any more and I felt small and naked as a new-hatched bird—alone upon the great river, the servant of the gods.

Yet, after a while, my eyes were opened and I saw. I saw both banks of the river—I saw that once there had been god-roads across it, though now they were broken and fallen like broken vines. Very great they were, and wonderful and broken—broken in the time of the Great Burning when the fire fell out of the sky. And always the current took me nearer to the Place of the Gods, and the huge ruins rose before my eyes.

I do not know the customs of rivers—we are the People of the Hills. I tried to guide my raft with the pole but it spun around. I thought the river meant to take me past the Place of the Gods and out into the Bitter Water of the legends. I grew angry then—my heart felt strong. I said aloud, "I am a priest and the son of a priest!" The gods heard me—they showed me how to paddle with the pole on one side of the raft. The current changed itself—I drew near to the Place of the Gods.

When I was very near, my raft struck and turned over. I can swim in our lakes—I swam to the shore. There was a great spike of rusted metal sticking out into the river—I hauled myself up upon it and sat there, panting. I had saved my bow and two arrows and the knife I found in the Dead Place but that was all. My raft went whirling downstream toward the Bitter Water. I looked after it, and thought if it had trod me under, at least I would be safely dead. Nevertheless, when I had dried my bowstring and re-strung it, I walked forward to the Place of the Gods.

It felt like ground underfoot; it did not burn me. It is not true what some of the tales say, that the ground there burns forever, for I have been there. Here and there were the marks and stains of the Great Burning, on the ruins, that is true. But they were old marks and old stains. It is not true either, what some of our priests say, that it is an island covered with fogs and enchantments. It is not. It is a great Dead Place—greater than any Dead Place we know. Everywhere in it there are god-roads, though most are cracked and broken. Everywhere there are the ruins of the high towers of the gods.

How shall I tell what I saw? I went carefully, my strung bow in my hand, my skin ready for danger. There should have been the wailings of spirits and the shrieks of demons, but there were not. It was very silent and sunny where I had landed—the wind and the rain and the birds that drop seeds had done their work—the grass grew in the cracks of the broken stone. It is a fair island—no wonder the gods built there. If I had come there, a god, I also would have built.

How shall I tell what I saw? The towers are not all broken—here and there one still stands, like a great tree in a forest, and the birds nest high. But the towers themselves look blind, for the gods are gone. I saw a fishhawk, catching fish in the river. I saw a little dance of white butterflies over a great heap of broken stones and columns. I went there and looked about me—there was a carved stone with cut—letters, broken in half. I can read letters but I could not understand these. They said UBTREAS. There was also the shattered image of a man or a god. It had been made of white stone and he wore his hair tied back like a woman's. His name was ASHING, as I read on the cracked half of a stone. I thought it wise to pray to ASHING, though I do not know that god.

How shall I tell what I saw? There was no smell of man left, on stone or metal. Nor were there many trees in that wilderness of stone. There are many pigeons, nesting and dropping in the towers—the gods must have loved them, or, perhaps, they used them for sacrifices. There are wild cats that roam the god-roads, green-eyed, unafraid of man. At night they wail like demons but they are not demons. The wild dogs are more dangerous, for they hunt in a pack, but them I did not meet till later. Everywhere there are the carved stones, carved with magical numbers or words.

I went north—I did not try to hide myself. When a god or a demon saw me, then I would die, but meanwhile I was no longer afraid. My hunger for knowledge burned in me—there was so much that I could not understand. After a while, I knew that my belly was hungry. I could have hunted for my meat, but I did not hunt. It is known that the gods did not hunt as we do—they got their food from enchanted boxes and jars. Sometimes these are still found in the Dead Places—once, when I was a child and foolish, I opened such a jar and tasted it and found the food sweet. But my father found out and punished me for it strictly, for, often, that food is death. Now, though, I had long gone past what was forbidden, and I entered the likeliest towers, looking for the food of the gods.

I found it at last in the ruins of a great temple in the mid-city. A mighty temple it must have been, for the roof was painted like the sky at night with its stars—that much I could see, though the colors were faint and dim. It went down into great caves and tunnels—perhaps they kept their slaves there. But when I started to climb down, I heard the squeaking of rats, so I did not go—rats are unclean, and there must have been many tribes of them, from the squeaking. But near there, I found food, in the heart of a ruin, behind a door that still opened. I ate only the fruits from the jars—they had a very sweet taste. There was drink, too, in bottles of glass—the drink of the gods was strong and made my head swim. After I had eaten and drunk, I slept on the top of a stone, my bow at my side.

When I woke, the sun was low. Looking down from where I lay, I saw a dog sitting on his haunches. His tongue was hanging out of his mouth; he looked as if he were laughing. He was a big dog, with a gray-brown coat, as big as a wolf. I sprang up and shouted at him but he did not move—he just sat there as if he were laughing. I did not like that. When I reached for a stone to throw, he moved swiftly out of the way of the stone. He was not afraid of me; he looked at me as if I were meat. No doubt I could have killed him with an arrow, but I did not know if there were others. Moreover, night was falling.

I looked about me—not far away there was a great, broken god-road, leading north. The towers were high enough, but not so high, and while many of the dead-houses were wrecked, there were some that stood. I went toward this god-road, keeping to the heights of the ruins, while the dog followed. When I had reached the god-road, I saw that there were others behind him. If I had slept later, they would have come upon me asleep and torn out my throat. As it was, they were sure enough of me; they did not hurry. When I went into the dead-house, they kept watch at the entrance—doubtless they thought they would have a fine hunt. But a dog cannot open a door and I knew, from the books, that the gods did not like to live on the ground but on high.

I had just found a door I could open when the dogs decided to rush. Ha! They were surprised when I shut the door in their faces—it was a good door, of strong metal. I could hear their foolish baying beyond it but I did not stop to answer them. I was in darkness—I found stairs and climbed. There were many stairs, turning around till my head was dizzy. At the top was another door—I found the knob and opened it. I was in a long small chamber—on one side of it was a bronze door that could not be opened, for it had no handle. Perhaps there was a magic word to open it but I did not have the word. I turned to the door in the opposite side of the wall. The lock of it was broken and I opened it and went in.

Within, there was a place of great riches. The god who lived there must have been a powerful god. The first room was a small ante-room—I waited there for some time, telling the spirits of the place that I came in peace and not as a robber. When it seemed to me that they had had time to hear me, I went on. Ah, what riches! Few, even, of the windows had been broken—it was all as it had been. The great windows that looked over the city had not been broken at all though they were dusty and streaked with many years. There were coverings on the floors, the colors not greatly faded, and the chairs were soft and deep. There were pictures upon the walls, very strange, very wonderful—I remember one of a bunch of flowers in a jar—if you came close to it, you could see nothing but bits of color, but if you stood away from it, the flowers might have been picked yesterday. It made my heart feel strange to look at this picture—and to look at the figure of a bird, in some hard clay, on a table and see it so like our birds. Everywhere there were books and writings, many in tongues that I could not read. The god who lived there must have been a wise god and full of knowledge. I felt I had a right there, as I sought knowledge also.

Nevertheless, it was strange. There was a washing-place but no water—perhaps the gods washed in air. There was a cooking-place but no wood, and though there was a machine to cook food, there was no place to put fire in it. Nor were there candles or lamps—there were things that looked like lamps but they had neither oil nor wick. All these things were magic, but I touched them and lived—the magic had gone out of them. Let me tell one thing to show. In the washing-place, a thing said "Hot" but it was not hot to the touch—another thing said "Cold" but it was not cold. This must have been a strong magic but the magic was gone. I do not understand—they had ways—I wish that I knew.

It was close and dry and dusty in the house of the gods. I have said the magic was gone but that is not true—it had gone from the magic things but it had not gone from the place. I felt the spirits about me, weighing upon me. Nor had I ever slept in a Dead Place before—and yet, tonight, I must sleep there. When I thought of it, my tongue felt dry in my throat, in spite of my wish for knowledge. Almost I would have gone down again and faced the dogs, but I did not.

I had not gone through all the rooms when the darkness fell. When it fell, I went back to the big room looking over the city and made fire. There was a place to make fire and a box with wood in it, though I do not think they cooked there. I wrapped myself in a floor-covering and slept in front of the fire—I was very tired.

Now I tell what is very strong magic. I woke in the midst of the night. When I woke, the fire had gone out and I was cold. It seemed to me that all around me there were whisperings and voices. I closed my eyes to shut them out. Some will say that I slept again, but I do not think that I slept. I could feel the spirits drawing my spirit out of my body as a fish is drawn on a line.

Why should I lie about it? I am a priest and the son of a priest. If there are spirits, as they say, in the small Dead Places near us, what spirits must there not be in that great Place of the Gods? And would not they wish to speak? After such long years? I know that I felt myself drawn as a fish is drawn on a line. I had stepped out of my body—I could see my body asleep in front of the cold fire, but it was not I. I was drawn to look out upon the city of the gods.

It should have been dark, for it was night, but it was not dark. Everywhere there were lights—lines of light—circles and blurs of light—ten thousand torches would not have been the same. The sky itself was alight—you could barely see the stars for the glow in the sky. I thought to myself "This is strong magic" and trembled. There was a roaring in my ears like the rushing of rivers. Then my eyes grew used to the light and my ears to the sound. I knew that I was seeing the city as it had been when the gods were alive.

That was a sight indeed—yes, that was a sight: I could not have seen it in the body—my body would have died. Everywhere went the gods, on foot and in chariots—there were gods beyond number and counting and their chariots blocked the streets. They had turned night to day for their pleasure-they did not sleep with the sun. The noise of their coming and going was the noise of the many waters. It was magic what they could do—it was magic what they did.

I looked out of another window—the great vines of their bridges were mended and god-roads went east and west. Restless, restless, were the gods and always in motion! They burrowed tunnels under rivers—they flew in the air. With unbelievable tools they did giant works—no part of the earth was safe from them, for, if they wished for a thing, they summoned it from the other side of the world. And always, as they labored and rested, as they feasted and made love, there was a drum in their ears—the pulse of the giant city, beating and beating like a man's heart.

Were they happy? What is happiness to the gods? They were great, they were mighty, they were wonderful and terrible. As I looked upon them and their magic, I felt like a child—but a little more, it seemed to me, and they would pull down the moon from the sky. I saw them with wisdom beyond wisdom and knowledge beyond knowledge. And yet not all they did was well done—even I could see that ? and yet their wisdom could not but grow until all was peace.

Then I saw their fate come upon them and that was terrible past speech. It came upon them as they walked the streets of their city. I have been in the fights with the Forest People—I have seen men die. But this was not like that. When gods war with gods, they use weapons we do not know. It was fire falling out of the sky and a mist that poisoned. It was the time of the Great Burning and the Destruction. They ran about like ants in the streets of their city—poor gods, poor gods! Then the towers began to fall. A few escaped—yes, a few. The legends tell it. But, even after the city had become a Dead Place, for many years the poison was still in the ground. I saw it happen, I saw the last of them die. It was darkness over the broken city and I wept.

All this, I saw. I saw it as I have told it, though not in the body. When I woke in the morning, I was hungry, but I did not think first of my hunger for my heart was perplexed and confused. I knew the reason for the Dead Places but I did not see why it had happened. It seemed to me it should not have happened, with all the magic they had. I went through the house looking for an answer. There was so much in the house I could not understand—and yet I am a priest and the son of a priest. It was like being on one side of the great river, at night, with no light to show the way.

Then I saw the dead god. He was sitting in his chair, by the window, in a room I had not entered before and, for the first moment, I thought that he was alive. Then I saw the skin on the back of his hand—it was like dry leather. The room was shut, hot and dry—no doubt that had kept him as he was. At first I was afraid to approach him—then the fear left me. He was sitting looking out over the city—he was dressed in the clothes of the gods. His age was neither young nor old—I could not tell his age. But there was wisdom in his face and great sadness. You could see that he would have not run away. He had sat at his window, watching his city die—then he himself had died. But it is better to lose one's life than one's spirit—and you could see from the face that his spirit had not been lost. I knew, that, if I touched him, he would fall into dust—and yet, there was something unconquered in the face.

That is all of my story, for then I knew he was a man—I knew then that they had been men, neither gods nor demons. It is a great knowledge, hard to tell and believe. They were men—they went a dark road, but they were men. I had no fear after that—I had no fear going home, though twice I fought off the dogs and once I was hunted for two days by the Forest People. When I saw my father again, I prayed and was purified. He touched my lips and my breast, he said, "You went away a boy. You come back a man and a priest." I said, "Father, they were men! I have been in the Place of the Gods and seen it! Now slay me, if it is the law—but still I know they were men."

He looked at me out of both eyes. He said, "The law is not always the same shape—you have done what you have done. I could not have done it my time, but you come after me. Tell!"

I told and he listened. After that, I wished to tell all the people but he showed me otherwise. He said, "Truth is a hard deer to hunt. If you eat too much truth at once, you may die of the truth. It was not idly that our fathers forbade the Dead Places." He was right—it is better the truth should come little by little. I have learned that, being a priest. Perhaps, in the old days, they ate knowledge too fast.

Nevertheless, we make a beginning. it is not for the metal alone we go to the Dead Places now—there are the books and the writings. They are hard to learn. And the magic tools are broken—but we can look at them and wonder. At least, we make a beginning. And, when I am chief priest we shall go beyond the great river. We shall go to the Place of the Gods—the place newyork—not one man but a company. We shall look for the images of the gods and find the god ASHING and the others—the gods Lincoln and Biltmore and Moses. But they were men who built the city, not gods or demons. They were men. I remember the dead man's face. They were men who were here before us. We must build again.

The Curfew Tolls

(1935)

"It is not enough to be the possessor of genius—the time and the man must conjoin. An Alexander the Great, born into an age of profound peace, might scarce have troubled the world—a Newton, grown up in a thieves' den, might have devised little but a new and ingenious picklock...."

Diversions of Historical Thought by
John Cleveland Cotton.

(The following extracts have been made from the letters of General Sir Charles William Geoffrey Estcourt, C.B., to his sister Harriet, Countess of Stokely, by permission of the Stokely family. Omissions are indicated by triple dots, thus ...)

St. Philippe-des-Bains, September 3d, 1788.

My dear sister: ... I could wish that my excellent Paris physician had selected some other spot for my convalescence. But he swears by the waters of St. Philip and I swear by him, so I must resign myself to a couple of yawning months ere my constitution mends. Nevertheless, you will get long letters from me, though I fear they may be dull ones. I cannot bring you the gossip of Baden or Aix—except for its baths, St. Philip is but one of a dozen small white towns on this agreeable coast. It has its good inn and its bad inn, its dusty, little square with its dusty, flea-bitten beggar, its posting-station and its promenade of scrubby lindens and palms. From the heights one may see Corsica on a clear day, and the Mediterranean is of an unexampled blue. To tell the truth, it is all agreeable enough, and an old Indian campaigner, like myself, should not complain. I am well treated at the Cheval Blanc—am I not an English milord?—and my excellent Gaston looks after me devotedly. But there is a blue-bottle drowsiness about small watering places out of season, and our gallant enemies, the French, know how to bore themselves more exquisitely in their provinces than any nation on earth. Would you think that the daily arrival of the diligence from Toulon would be an excitement? Yet it is to me, I assure you, and to all St. Philip. I walk, I take the waters, I read Ossian, I play piquet with Gaston, and yet I seem to myself but half-alive....

...You will smile and say to me, "Dear brother, you have always plumed yourself on being a student of human nature. Is there no society, no character for you to study, even in St. Philippe-des-Bains?" My dear sister, I bend myself earnestly to that end, yet so far with little result. I have talked to my doctor—a good man but unpolished; I have talked to the curé—a good man but dull. I have even attempted the society of the baths, beginning with Monsieur le Marquis de la Percedragon, who has ninety-six quarterings, soiled wristbands, and a gloomy interest in my liver, and ending with Mrs. Macgregor Jenkins, a worthy and red-faced lady whose conversation positively cannonades with dukes and duchesses. But, frankly, I prefer my chair in the garden and my Ossian to any of them, even at the risk of being considered a bear. A witty scoundrel would be the veriest godsend to me, but do such exist in St. Philip? I trow not. As it is, in my weakened condition, I am positively agog when Gaston comes in every morning with his budget of village scandal. A pretty pass to come to, you will say, for a man who has served with Eyre Coote and but for the mutabilities of fortune, not to speak of a most damnable cabal ... (A long passage dealing with General Estcourt's East Indian services and his personal and unfavorable opinion of Warren Hastings is here omitted from the manuscript.) ... But, at fifty, a man is either a fool or a philosopher. Nevertheless, unless Gaston provides me with a character to try my wits on, shortly, I shall begin to believe that they too have deteriorated with Indian suns....

September 21st, 1788.

My Dear Sister: ... Believe me, there is little soundness in the views of your friend, Lord Martindale. The French monarchy is not to be compared with our own, but King Louis is an excellent and well-beloved prince, and the proposed summoning of the States-General cannot but have the most salutary effect. ... (Three pages upon French politics and the possibility of cultivating sugar-cane in Southern France are here omitted.) ... As for news of myself, I continue my yawning course, and feel a decided improvement from the waters.... So I shall continue them though the process is slow....

You ask me, I fear a trifle mockingly, how my studies in human nature proceed?

Not so ill, my dear sister—I have, at least, scraped acquaintance with one odd fish, and that, in St. Philip, is a triumph. For some time, from my chair in the promenade, I have observed a pursy little fellow, of my age or thereabouts, stalking up and down between the lindens. His company seems avoided by such notables of the place as Mrs. Macgregor Jenkins and at first I put him down as a retired actor, for there is something a little theatrical in his dress and walk. He wears a wide-brimmed hat of straw, loose nankeen trousers and a quasi-military coat, and takes his waters with as much ceremony as Monsieur le Marquis, though not quite with the same *ton*. I should put him down as a Meridional, for he has the quick, dark eye, the sallow skin, the corpulence and the rodomontish airs that mark your true son of the Midi, once he has passed his lean and hungry youth.

And yet, there is some sort of unsuccessful oddity about him, which sets him off from your successful bourgeois. I cannot put my finger on it yet, but it interests me.

At any rate, I was sitting in my accustomed chair, reading Ossian, this morning, as he made his solitary rounds of the promenade. Doubtless I was more than usually absorbed in my author, for I must have pronounced some lines aloud as he passed. He gave me a quick glance at the time, but nothing more. But on his next round, as he was about to pass me, he hesitated for a moment, stopped, and then, removing his straw hat, saluted me very civilly.

"Monsieur will pardon me," he said, with a dumpy hauteur, "but surely monsieur is English? And surely the lines that monsieur just repeated are from the great poet, Ossian?"

I admitted both charges, with a smile, and he bowed again.

"Monsieur will excuse the interruption," he said, "but I myself have long admired the poetry of Ossian"—and with that he continued my quotation to the end of the passage, in very fair English, too, though with a strong accent. I complimented him, of course, effusively—after all, it is not every day that one runs across a fellow-admirer of Ossian on the promenade of a small French watering place—and after that, he sat down in the chair beside me and we fell into talk. He seems, astonishingly for a Frenchman, to have an excellent acquaintance with our English poets—perhaps he has been a tutor in some English family. I did not press him with questions on this first encounter, though I noted that he spoke French with a slight accent also, which seems odd.

There is something a little rascally about him, to tell you the truth, though his conversation with me was both forceful and elevated. An ill man, too, and a disappointed one, or I miss my mark, yet his eyes, when he talks, are strangely animating. I fancy I would not care to meet him in a *guet-apens*, and yet, he may be the most harmless of broken pedagogues. We took a glass of waters together, to the great disgust of Mrs. Macgregor Jenkins, who ostentatiously drew her skirts aside. She let me know, afterward, in so many words, that my acquaintance was a noted bandit, though, when pressed, she could give no better reason than that he lives a little removed from the town, that "nobody knows where he comes from" and that his wife is "no better than she should be," whatever that portentous phrase entails. Well, one would hardly call him a gentleman, even by Mrs. Macgregor's somewhat easy standards, but he has given me better conversation than I have had in a month—and if he is a bandit, we might discuss thuggee together. But I hope for nothing so stimulating, though I must question Gaston about him....

October 11th.

But Gaston could tell me little, except that my acquaintance comes from Sardinia or some such island originally, has served in the French army and is popularly supposed to possess the evil eye. About Madame he hinted that he could tell me a great deal, but I did not labor the point. After all, if my friend has been c-ck-ld-d—do not blush, my dear sister!—that, too, is the portion of a philosopher, and I find his wide range of conversation much more palatable than Mrs. Macgregor Jenkins' rewarmed London gossip. Nor has he tried to borrow money from me yet, something which, I am frank to say, I expected and was prepared to refuse....

November 20th.

...Triumph! My character is found—and a character of the first water, I assure you! I have dined with him in his house, and a very bad dinner it was. Madame is not a good housekeeper, whatever else she may be. And what she has been, one can see at a glance—she has all the little faded coquetries of the garrison coquette. Good-tempered, of course, as such women often are, and must have been pretty in her best days, though with shocking bad teeth. I suspect her of a touch of the tarbrush, though there I may be wrong. No doubt she caught my friend young—I have seen the same thing happen in India often enough—the experienced woman and the youngster fresh from England. Well, 'tis an old story—an old one with him, too—and no doubt Madame has her charms, though she is obviously one reason why he has not risen.

After dinner, Madame departed, not very willingly, and he took me into his study for a chat. He had even procured a bottle of port, saying he knew the Englishman's taste for it, and while it was hardly the right Cockburn, I felt touched by the attention. The man is desperately lonely—one reads that in his big eyes. He is also desperately proud, with the quick, touchy sensitiveness of the failure, and I quite exerted myself to draw him out.

And indeed, the effort repaid me. His own story is simple enough. He is neither bandit nor pedagogue, but, like myself, a broken soldier—a major of the French Royal Artillery, retired on half pay for some years. I think it creditable of him to have reached so respectable a rank, for he is of foreign birth—Sardinian, I think I told you—and the French service is by no means as partial to foreigners as they were in the days of the first Irish Brigade. Moreover, one simply does not rise in that service, unless one is a gentleman of quarterings, and that he could hardly claim. But the passion of his life has been India, and that is what interests me. And, 'pon my honor, he was rather astonishing about it.

As soon as, by a lucky chance, I hit upon the subject, his eyes lit up and his sickness dropped away. Pretty soon he began to take maps from a cabinet in the wall and ply me with questions about my own small experiences. And very soon indeed, I am abashed to state, I found myself stumbling in my answers. It was all book knowledge on his part, of course, but where the devil he could have got some of it, I do not know. Indeed, he would even correct me, now and then, as cool as you please. "Eight twelve pounders, I think, on the north wall of the old fortifications of Madras—" and the deuce of it is, he would be right. Finally, I could contain myself no longer.

"But, major, this is incredible," I said. "I have served twenty years with John Company and thought that I had some knowledge. But one would say you had fought over every inch of Bengal!"

He gave me a quick look, almost of anger, and began to roll up his maps.

"So I have, in my mind," he said, shortly, "but, as my superiors have often informed me, my hobby is a tedious one."

"It is not tedious to me," I said boldly. "Indeed, I have often marveled at your government's neglect of their opportunities in India. True, the issue is settled now—"

"It is by no means settled," he said, interrupting me rudely. I stared at him.

"It was settled, I believe, by Baron Clive, at a spot named Plassey," I said frigidly. "And afterward, by my own old general, Eyre Coote, at another spot named Wandewash."

"Oh, yes—yes—yes," he said impatiently, "I grant you Clive—Clive was a genius and met the fate of geniuses. He steals an empire for you, and your virtuous English Parliament holds up its hands in horror because he steals a few lakhs of rupees for himself as well. So he blows out his brains in disgrace—you inexplicable English!—and you lose your genius. A great pity. I would not have treated Clive so. But then, if I had been Milord Clive, I would not have blown out my brains."

"And what would you have done, had you been Clive?" I said, for the man's calm, staring conceit amused me.

His eyes were dangerous for a moment and I saw why the worthy Mrs. Macgregor Jenkins had called him a bandit.

"Oh," he said coolly, "I would have sent a file of grenadiers to your English Parliament and told it to hold its tongue. As Cromwell did. Now there was a man. But your Clive—faugh!—he had the ball at his feet and he refused to kick it. I withdraw the word genius. He was a nincompoop. At the least, he might have made himself a rajah."

This was a little too much, as you may imagine. "General Clive had his faults," I said icily, "but he was a true Briton and a patriot."

"He was a fool," said my puffy little major, flatly, his lower lip stuck out. "As big a fool as Dupleix, and that is saying much. Oh, some military skill, some talent for organization, yes. But a genius would have brushed him into the sea! It was possible to hold Arcot, it was possible to win Plassey—look!" and, with that, he ripped another map from his cabinet and began to expound to me eagerly exactly what he would have done in command of the French forces in India, in 1757, when he must have been but a lad in his twenties. He thumped the paper, he strewed corks along the table for his troops—corks taken from a supply in a tin box, so it must be an old game with him. And, as I listened, my irritation faded, for the man's monomania was obvious. Nor was it, to tell the truth, an ill-designed plan of campaign, for corks on a map. Of course these things are different, in the field.

I could say, with honesty, that his plan had features of novelty, and he gulped the words down hungrily—he has a great appetite for flattery.

"Yes, yes," he said. "That is how it should be done—the thickest skull can see it. And, ill as I am, with a fleet and ten thousand picked men—" He dreamed, obviously, the sweat of his exertions on his waxy face—it was absurd and yet touching to see him dream.

"You would find a certain amount of opposition," I said, in an amused voice.

"Oh, yes, yes," he said quickly, "I do not underrate the English. Excellent horse, solid foot. But no true knowledge of cannon, and I am a gunner—"

I hated to bring him down to earth and yet I felt that I must.

"Of course, major," I said, "you have had great experience in the field."

He looked at me for a moment, his arrogance quite unshaken.

"I have had very little," he said, quietly, "but one knows how the thing should be done or one does not know. And that is enough."

He stared at me for an instant with his big eyes. A little mad, of course. And yet I found myself saying, "But surely, major—what happened?"

"Why," he said, still quietly, "what happens to folk who have naught but their brains to sell? I staked my all on India when I was young—I thought that my star shone over it. I ate dirty puddings—*corpo di Baccho!*—to get there—I was no De Rohan or Soubise to win the king's favor! And I reached there indeed, in my youth, just in time to be included in the surrender of Pondicherry." He laughed, rather terribly, and sipped at his glass.

"You English were very courteous captors," he said. "But I was not released till the Seven Years War had ended—that was in '63. Who asks for the special exchange of an unknown artillery lieutenant? And then ten years odd of garrison duty at Mauritius. It was there that I met Madame—she is a Creole. A pleasant spot, Mauritius. We used to fire the cannon at the sea birds when we had enough ammunition for target practice," and he chuckled drearily. "By then I was thirty-seven. They had to make me a captain—they even brought me back to France. To garrison duty. I have been on garrison duty, at Toulon, at Brest, at—" He ticked off the names on his fingers but I did not like his voice.

"But surely," I said, "the American war, though a small affair—there were opportunities—"

"And who did they send?" he said quickly. "Lafayette—Rochambeau—De Grasse—the sprigs of the nobility. Oh, at Lafayette's age, I would have volunteered like Lafayette. But one should be successful in youth—after that, the spring is broken. And when one is over forty, one has responsibilities. I have a large family, you see, though not of my own begetting," and he chuckled as if at a secret joke. "Oh, I wrote the Continental Congress," he said reflectively, "but they preferred a dolt like Von Steuben. A good dolt, an honest dolt, but there you have it. I also wrote your British War Office," he said in an even voice. "I must show you that plan of campaign—sometime—they could have crushed General Washington with it in three weeks."

I stared at him, a little appalled.

"For an officer who has taken his king's shilling to send to an enemy nation a plan for crushing his own country's ally," I said, stiffly—" well, in England, we would call that treason."

"And what is treason?" he said lightly. "If we call it unsuccessful ambition we shall be nearer the truth." He looked at me, keenly. "You are shocked, General Estcourt," he said. "I am sorry for that. But have you never known the curse"—and his voice vibrated—"the curse of not being employed when you should be employed? The curse of being a hammer with no nail to drive? The curse—the curse of sitting in a dusty garrison town with dreams that would split the brain of a Caesar, and no room on earth for those dreams?"

"Yes," I said, unwillingly, for there was something in him that demanded the truth, "I have known that."

"Then you know hells undreamed of by the Christian," he said, with a sigh, "and if I committed treason—well, I have been punished for it. I might have been a brigadier, otherwise—I had Choiseul's ear for a few weeks, after great labor. As it is, I am here on half pay, and there will not be another war in my time. Moreover, M. de Ségur has proclaimed that all officers now must show sixteen quarterings. Well, I wish them joy of those officers, in the next conflict. Meanwhile, I have my corks, my maps and my family ailment." He smiled and tapped his side. "It killed my father at thirty-nine—it has not treated me quite so ill, but it will come for me soon enough."

And indeed, when I looked at him, I could well believe it, for the light had gone from his eyes and his cheeks were flabby. We chatted a little on indifferent subjects after that, then I left him, wondering whether to pursue the acquaintance. He is indubitably a character, but some of his speeches leave a taste in my mouth. Yet he can be greatly attractive—even now, with his mountainous failure like a cloak upon him. And yet why should I call it mountainous? His conceit is mountainous enough, but what else could he have expected of his career? Yet I wish I could forget his eyes.... To tell the truth, he puzzles me and I mean to get to the bottom of him....

February 12th, 1789.

...I have another sidelight on the character of my friend, the major. As I told you, I was half of a mind to break off the acquaintance entirely, but he came up to me so civilly, the following day, that I could find no excuse. And since then, he has made me no embarrassingly treasonable confidences, though whenever we discuss the art of war, his arrogance is unbelievable.

He even informed me, the other day, that while Frederick of Prussia was a fair general, his tactics might have been improved upon. I merely laughed and turned the question. Now and then I play a war game with him, with his corks and maps, and when I let him win, he is as pleased as a child.... His illness increases visibly, despite the waters, and he shows an eagerness for my company which I cannot but find touching.... After all, he is a man of intelligence, and the company he has had to keep must have galled him at times....

Now and then I amuse myself by speculating what might have happened to him, had he chosen some other profession than that of arms. He has, as I have told you, certain gifts of the actor, yet his stature and figure must have debarred him from tragic parts, while he certainly does not possess the humors of the comedian. Perhaps his best choice would have been the Romish church, for there, the veriest fisherman may hope, at least, to succeed to the keys of St. Peter.... And yet, Heaven knows, he would have made a very bad priest!...

But, to my tale. I had missed him from our accustomed walks for some days and went to his house—St. Helen's it is called; we live in a pother of saints' names hereabouts—one evening to inquire. I did not hear the quarreling voices till the tousle-haired servant had admitted me and then it was too late to retreat. Then my friend bounced down the corridor, his sallow face bored and angry.

"Ah, General Estcourt!" he said, with a complete change of expression as soon as he saw me. "What fortune! I was hoping you would pay us a call—I wish to introduce you to my family!"

He had told me previously of his pair of stepchildren by Madame's first marriage, and I must confess I felt curious to see them. But it was not of them he spoke, as I soon gathered.

"Yes," he said. "My brothers and sisters, or most of them,

are here for a family council. You come in the nick of time!" He pinched my arm and his face glowed with the malicious naïveté of a child. "They do not believe that I really know an English general—it will be a great blow to them!" he whispered as we passed down the corridor. "Ah, if you had only worn your uniform and your Garters! But one cannot have everything in life!"

Well, my dear sister, what a group, when we entered the salon! It is a small room, tawdrily furnished in the worst French taste, with a jumble of Madame's femininities and souvenirs from the Island of Mauritius, and they were all sitting about in the French after-dinner fashion, drinking tisane and quarreling. And, indeed, had the room been as long as the nave of St. Peter's, it would yet have seemed too small for such a crew! An old mother, straight as a ramrod and as forbidding, with the burning eyes and the bitter dignity one sees on the faces of certain Italian peasants—you could see that they were all a little afraid of her except my friend, and he, I must say, treated her with a filial courtesy that was greatly to his credit. Two sisters, one fattish, swarthy and spiteful, the other with the wreck of great beauty and the evident marks of a certain profession on her shabby-fine *toilette* and her pinkened cheeks. An innkeeper brother-in-law called Buras or Durat, with a jowlish, heavily handsome face and the manners of a cavalry sergeant—he is married to the spiteful sister. And two brothers, one sheep-like, one fox-like, yet both bearing a certain resemblance to my friend.

The sheep-like brother is at least respectable, I gathered—a provincial lawyer in a small way of business whose great pride is that he has actually appeared before the Court of Appeals at Marseilles. The other, the fox-like one, makes his living more dubiously—he seems the sort of fellow who orates windily in taprooms about the Rights of Man, and other nonsense of M. Rousseau's. I would certainly not trust him with my watch, though he is trying to get himself elected to the States-General. And, as regards family concord, it was obvious at first glance that not one of them trusted the others. And yet, that is not all of the tribe. There are, if you will believe me, two other brothers living, and this family council was called to deal with the affairs of the next-to-youngest, who seems, even in this mélange, to be a black sheep.

I can assure you, my head swam, and when my friend introduced me, proudly, as a Knight of the Garters, I did not even bother to contradict him. For they admitted me to their intimate circle at once—there was no doubt about that. Only the old lady remained aloof, saying little and sipping her camomile tea as if it were the blood of her enemies. But, one by one, the others related to me, with an unasked-for frankness, the most intimate and scandalous details of their brothers' and sisters' lives. They seemed united only on two points, jealousy of my friend, the major, because he is his mother's favorite, and dislike of Madame Josephine because she gives herself airs. Except for the haggard beauty—I must say, that, while her remarks anent her sister-in-law were not such as I would care to repeat, she seemed genuinely fond of her brother, the major, and expounded his virtues to me through an overpowering cloud of scent.

It was like being in a nest of Italian smugglers, or a den of quarrelsome foxes, for they all talked, or rather barked at once, even the brother-in-law, and only Madame Mère could bring silence among them. And yet, my friend enjoyed it. It was obvious he showed them off before me as he might have displayed the tricks of a set of performing animals. And yet with a certain fondness, too—that is the inexplicable part of it. I do not know which sentiment was upmost in my mind—respect for this family feeling or pity for his being burdened with such a clan.

For though not the eldest, he is the strongest among them,

and they know it. They rebel, but he rules their family conclaves like a petty despot. I could have laughed at the farce of it, and yet, it was nearer tears. For here, at least, my friend was a personage.

I got away as soon as I could, despite some pressing looks from the haggard beauty. My friend accompanied me to the door.

"Well, well," he said, chuckling and rubbing his hands, "I am infinitely obliged to you, general. They will not forget this in a hurry. Before you entered, Joseph"—Joseph is the sheep-like one—"was boasting about his acquaintance with a *sous-intendant*, but an English general, bah! Joseph will have green eyes for a fortnight!" And he rubbed his hands again in a perfect paroxysm of delight.

It was too childlike to make me angry. "I am glad, of course, to have been of any service," I said.

"Oh, you have been a great service," he said. "They will not plague my poor Josie for at least half an hour. Ah, this is a bad business of Louis'—a bad business!"—Louis is the black sheep—"but we will patch it up somehow. Hortense is worth three of him—he must go back to Hortense!"

"You have a numerous family, major," I said, for want of something better to say.

"Oh, yes," he said, cheerfully. "Pretty numerous—I am sorry you could not meet the others. Though Louis is a fool—I pampered him in his youth. Well! He was a baby—and Jerome a mule. Still, we haven't done so badly for ourselves; not badly. Joseph makes a go of his law practice—there are fools enough in the world to be impressed by Joseph—and if Lucien gets to the States-General, you may trust Lucien to feather his nest! And there are the grandchildren, and a little money—not much," he said, quickly. "They mustn't expect that from me. But it's a step up from where we started—if papa had lived, he wouldn't have been so ill-pleased. Poor Elisa's gone, but the rest of us have stuck together, and, while we may seem a little rough, to strangers, our hearts are in the right place. When I was a boy," and he chuckled again, "I had other ambitions for them. I thought, with luck on my side, I could make them all kings and queens. Funny, isn't it, to think of a numskull like Joseph as a king! Well, that was the boy of it. But, even so, they'd all be eating chestnuts back on the island without me, and that's something."

He said it rather defiantly, and I did not know which to marvel at most—his preposterous pride in the group or his cool contempt of them. So I said nothing but shook his hand instead. I could not help doing the latter. For surely, if anyone started in life with a millstone about his neck ... and yet they are none of them ordinary people....

March 13th, 1789.

...My friend's complaint has taken a turn for the worse and it is I who pay him visits now. It is the act of a Christian to do so and, to tell the truth, I have become oddly attached to him, though I can give no just reason for the attachment. He makes a bad patient, by the way, and is often abominably rude to both myself and Madame, who nurses him devotedly though unskillfully. I told him yesterday that I could have no more of it and he looked at me with his strangely luminous eyes. "So," he said, "even the English desert the dying." ... Well, I stayed; after that, what else might a gentleman do? ... Yet I cannot feel that he bears me any real affection—he exerts himself to charm, on occasion, but one feels he is playing a game ... yes, even upon his deathbed, he plays a game ... a complex character....

April 28th, 1789.

...My friend the major's malady approaches its term—the last few days find him fearfully enfeebled. He knows that the end draws nigh; indeed he speaks of it often, with remarkable calmness. I had thought it might turn his mind toward religion, but while he has accepted the ministrations of his Church, I fear it is without the sincere repentance of a Christian. When the priest had left him, yesterday, he summoned me, remarking, "Well, all that is over with," rather more in the tone of a man who has just reserved a place in a coach than one who will shortly stand before his Maker.

"It does no harm," he said, reflectively. "And, after all, it might be true. Why not?" and he chuckled in a way that repelled me. Then he asked me to read to him—not the Bible, as I had expected, but some verses of the poet Gray. He listened attentively, and when I came to the passage, "Hands, that the rod of empire might have swayed," and its successor, "Some mute inglorious Milton here may rest," he asked me to repeat them. When I had done so, he said, "Yes, yes. That is true, very true. I did not think so in boyhood—I thought genius must force its own way. But your poet is right about it."

I found this painful, for I had hoped that his illness had brought him to a juster, if less arrogant, estimate of his own abilities.

"Come, major," I said, soothingly, "we cannot all be great men, you know. And you have no need to repine. After all, as you say, you have risen in the world—"

"Risen?" he said, and his eyes flashed. "Risen? Oh, God, that I should die alone with my one companion an Englishman with a soul of suet! Fool, if I had had Alexander's chance, I would have bettered Alexander! And it will come, too, that is the worst of it. Already Europe is shaking with a new birth. If I had been born under the Sun-King, I would be a Marshal of France; if I had been born twenty years ago, I would mold a new Europe with my fists in the next half-dozen years. Why did they put my soul in my body at this infernal time? Do you not understand, imbecile? Is there no one who understands?"

I called Madame at this, as he was obviously delirious, and, after some trouble, we got him quieted.

May 8th, 1789.

...My poor friend is gone, and peacefully enough at the last. His death, oddly enough, coincided with the date of the opening of the States-General at Versailles. The last moments of life are always painful for the observer, but his end was as relatively serene as might be hoped for, considering his character. I was watching at one side of the bed and a thunderstorm was raging at the time. No doubt, to his expiring consciousness, the cracks of the thunder sounded like artillery, for, while we were waiting the death-struggle, he suddenly raised himself in the bed and listened intently. His eyes glowed, a beatific expression passed over his features. "The army! Head of the army!" he whispered ecstatically, and, when we caught him, he was lifeless ... I must say that, while it may not be very Christian, I am glad that death brought him what life could not, and that, in the very article of it, he saw himself at the head of victorious troops. Ah, Fame—delusive spectre ... (A page of disquisition by General Estcourt on the vanities of human ambition is here omitted.) ... The face, after death, was composed, with a certain majesty, even... one could see that he might have been handsome as a youth....

May 26th, 1789.

... I shall return to Paris by easy stages and reach Stokely sometime in June. My health is quite restored and all that has kept me here this long has been the difficulty I have met with in attempting to settle my poor friend, the major's affairs. For one thing, he appears to have been originally a native of Corsica, not of Sardinia as I had thought, and while that explains much in his character, it has also given occupation to the lawyers. I have met his rapacious family, individually and in conclave, and, if there are further gray hairs on my head, you may put it down to them.... However, I have finally assured the major's relict of her legitimate rights in his estate, and that is something—my one ray of comfort in the matter being the behavior of her son by the former marriage, who seems an excellent and virtuous young man....

...You will think me a very soft fellow, no doubt, for wasting so much time upon a chance acquaintance who was neither, in our English sense, a gentleman nor a man whose Christian virtues counterbalanced his lack of true breeding. Yet there was a tragedy about him beyond his station, and that verse of Gray's rings in my head. I wish I could forget the expression on his face when he spoke of it. Suppose a genius born in circumstances that made the development of that genius impossible—well, all this is the merest moonshine....

... To revert to more practical matters, I discover that the major has left me his military memoirs, papers and commentaries, including his maps. Heaven knows what I shall do with them! I cannot, in courtesy, burn them *sur-le-champ*, and yet they fill two huge packing cases and the cost of transporting them to Stokely will be considerable. Perhaps I will take them to Paris and quietly dispose of them there to some waste-paper merchant.... In return for this unsought legacy, Madame has consulted me in regard to a stone and epitaph for her late husband, and, knowing that otherwise the family would squabble over the affair for weeks, I have drawn up a design which I hope meets with their approval. It appears that he particularly desired that the epitaph should be writ in English, saying that France had had enough of him, living—a freak of dying vanity for which one must pardon him. However, I have produced the following, which I hope will answer.

Here lies
NAPOLEONE BUONAPARTE
Major of the Royal Artillery
of France.
Born August 15th, 1737
at Ajaccio, Corsica.
Died May 5th, 1789
at St. Philippe-des-Bains
"Rest, perturbed spirit …"

…I had thought, for some hours, of excerpting the lines of Gray's—the ones that still ring in my head. But, on reflection, though they suit well enough, they yet seem too cruel to the dust.

The King of the Cats
(1929)

"But, my *dear*," said Mrs. Culverin, with a tiny gasp, "you can't actually mean a *tail!*"

Mrs. Dingle nodded impressively. "Exactly. I've seen him. Twice. Paris, of course, and then, a command appearance at Rome—we were in the Royal box. He conducted my dear, you've never heard such effects from an orchestra—and, my dear," she hesitated slightly, "he conducted *with* it."

"How perfectly, fascinatingly too horrid for words!" said Mrs. Culverin in a dazed but greedy voice. "We *must* have him to dinner as soon as he comes over—he is coming over, isn't he?"

"The twelfth," said Mrs. Dingle with a gleam in her eyes. "The New Symphony people have asked him to be guest-conductor for three special concerts—I do hope you can dine with us some night while he's here—he'll be very busy, of course—but he's promised to give us what time he can spare—"

"Oh, thank you, dear," said Mrs. Culverin, abstractedly, her last raid upon Mrs. Dingle's pet British novelist still fresh in her mind. "You're always so delightfully hospitable—but you mustn't wear yourself out the rest of us must do *our* part—I know Henry and myself would be only too glad to—"

"That's very sweet of you, darling." Mrs. Dingle also remembered the larceny of the British novelist. "But we're just going to give Monsieur Tibault—sweet name, isn't it! They say he's descended from the Tybalt in 'Romeo and Juliet' and that's why he doesn't like Shakespeare—we're just going to give Monsieur Tibault the simplest sort of time—a little reception after his first concert, perhaps. He hates," she looked around the table, "large, mixed parties. And then, of course, his—er—little idiosyncrasy—" she coughed delicately. "It makes him feel a trifle shy with strangers."

"But I don't understand yet, Aunt Emily," said Tommy Brooks, Mrs. Dingle's nephew. "Do you really mean this Tibault bozo has a tail? Like a monkey and everything?"

"Tommy dear," said Mrs. Culverin, crushingly, "in the first place Monsieur Tibault is not a bozo—he is a very distinguished musician—the finest conductor in Europe. And in the second place—"

"He has," Mrs. Dingle was firm. "He has a tail. He conducts with it."

"Oh, but honestly!" said Tommy, his ears pinkening. "I mean—of course, if you say so, Aunt Emily, I'm sure he has—but still, it sounds pretty steep, if you know what I mean! How about it, Professor Tatto?"

Professor Tatto cleared his throat. "Tck," he said, putting his fingertips together cautiously, "I shall be very anxious to see this Monsieur Tibault. For myself, I have never observed a genuine specimen of *homo caudatus*, so I should be inclined to doubt, and yet ... In the Middle Ages, for instance, the belief in men—er—tailed or with caudal appendages of some sort, was both widespread and, as far as we can gather, well-founded. As late as the Eighteenth Century, a Dutch sea-captain with some character for veracity recounts the discovery of a pair of such creatures in the island of Formosa. They were in a low state of civilization, I believe, but the appendages in question were quite distinct. And in 1860, Dr. Grimbrook, the English surgeon, claims to have treated no less than three African natives with short but evident tails—though his testimony rests upon his unsupported word. After all, the thing is not impossible, though doubtless unusual. Web feet—rudimentary gills—these occur with some frequency. The appendix we have with us always. The chain of our descent from the ape-like form is by no means complete. For that matter," he beamed around the table, "what can we call the last few vertebrae of the normal spine but the beginnings of a concealed and rudimentary tail? Oh, yes—yes—it's possible—quite—that in an extraordinary case—a reversion to type—a survival—though, of course—"

"I told you so," said Mrs. Dingle triumphantly. "*Isn't* it fascinating? Isn't it, Princess?"

The Princess Vivrakanarda's eyes, blue as a field of larkspur, fathomless as the centre of heaven, rested lightly for a moment on Mrs. Dingle's excited countenance.

"Ve-ry fascinating," she said, in a voice like stroked, golden velvet. "I should like I should like ve-ry much to meet this Monsieur Tibault."

"Well, *I* hope he breaks his neck!" said Tommy Brooks, under his breath but nobody ever paid much attention to Tommy.

Nevertheless as the time for Mr. Tibault's arrival in these States drew nearer and nearer, people in general began to wonder whether the Princess had spoken quite truthfully—for there was no doubt of the fact that, up till then, she had been the unique sensation of the season—and you know what social lions and lionesses are.

It was, if you remember, a Siamese season, and genuine Siamese were at quite as much of a premium as Russian accents had been in the quaint old days when the Chauve-Souris was a novelty. The Siamese Art Theatre, imported at terrific expense, was playing to packed houses. "Gushuptzgu," an epic novel of

Siamese farm life, in nineteen closely-printed volumes, had just been awarded the Nobel prize. Prominent pet-and-newt dealers reported no cessation in the appalling demand for Siamese cats. And upon the crest of this wave of interest in things Siamese, the Princess Vivrakanarda poised with the elegant nonchalance of a Hawaiian water-baby upon its surfboard. She was indispensable. She was incomparable. She was everywhere.

Youthful, enormously wealthy, allied on one hand to the Royal Family of Siam and on the other to the Cabots (and yet with the first eighteen of her twenty-one years shrouded from speculation in a golden zone of mystery), the mingling of races in her had produced an exotic beauty as distinguished as it was strange. She moved with a feline, effortless grace, and her skin was as if it had been gently powdered with tiny grains of the purest gold yet the blueness of her eyes, set just a trifle slantingly, was as pure and startling as the sea on the rocks of Maine. Her brown hair fell to her knees she had been offered extraordinary sums by the Master Barbers' Protective Association to have it shingled. Straight as a waterfall tumbling over brown rocks, it had a vague perfume of sandalwood and suave spices and held tints of rust and the sun. She did not talk very much—but then she did not have to—her voice had an odd, small, melodious huskiness that haunted the mind. She lived alone and was reputed to be very lazy—at least it was known that she slept during most of the day—but at night she bloomed like a moon-flower and a depth came into her eyes.

It was no wonder that Tommy Brooks fell in love with her. The wonder was that she let him. There was nothing exotic or distinguished about Tommy—he was just one of those pleasant, normal young men who seem created to carry on the bond business by reading the newspapers in the University Club during most of the day, and can always be relied upon at night to fill an unexpected hole in a dinner-party. It is true that the Princess could hardly be said to do more than tolerate any of her suitors—no one had ever seen those aloofly arrogant eyes enliven at the entrance of any male. But she seemed to be able to tolerate Tommy a little more than the rest—and that young man's infatuated day-dreams were beginning to be beset by smart solitaires and imaginary apartments on Park Avenue, when the famous M. Tibault conducted his first concert at Carnegie Hall.

Tommy Brooks sat beside the Princess. The eyes he turned upon her were eyes of longing and love, but her face was as impassive as a mask, and the only remark she made during the preliminary bustlings was that there seemed to be a number of people in the audience. But Tommy was relieved, if anything, to find her even a little more aloof than usual, for, ever since Mrs. Culverin's dinner-party, a vague disquiet as to the possible impression which this Tibault creature might make upon her had been growing in his mind. It shows his devotion that he was present at all. To a man whose simple Princetonian nature found in "Just a Little Love, a Little Kiss," the quintessence of musical art, the average symphony was a positive torture, and he looked forward to the evening's programme itself with a grim, brave smile.

"Ssh!" said Mrs. Dingle, breathlessly. "He's coming!" It seemed to the startled Tommy as if he were suddenly back in the trenches under a heavy barrage, as M. Tibault made his entrance to a perfect bombardment of applause.

Then the enthusiastic noise was sliced off in the middle and a gasp took its place—a vast, windy sigh, as if every person in that multitude had suddenly said, "Ah." For the papers had not lied about him. The tail was there.

They called him theatric—but how well he understood the

uses of theatricalism! Dressed in unrelieved black from head to foot (the black dress-shirt had been a special token of Mussolini's esteem), he did not walk on, he strolled, leisurely, easily, aloofly, the famous tail curled nonchalantly about one wrist—a suave, black panther lounging through a summer garden with that little mysterious weave of the head that panthers have when they pad behind bars—the glittering darkness of his eyes unmoved by any surprise or elation. He nodded, twice, in regal acknowledgment, as the clapping reached an apogee of frenzy. To Tommy there was something dreadfully reminiscent of the Princess in the way he nodded. Then he turned to his orchestra.

A second and louder gasp went up from the audience at this point, for, as he turned, the tip of that incredible tail twined with dainty carelessness into some hidden pocket and produced a black baton. But Tommy did not even notice. He was looking at the Princess instead.

She had not even bothered to clap, at first, but now—He had never seen her moved like this, never. She was not applauding, her hands were clenched in her lap, but her whole body was rigid, rigid as a steel bar, and the blue flowers of her eyes were bent upon the figure of M. Tibault in a terrible concentration. The pose of her entire figure was so still and intense that for an instant Tommy had the lunatic idea that any moment she might leap from her seat beside him as lightly as a moth, and land, with no sound, at M. Tibault's side to—yes—to rub her proud head against his coat in worship. Even Mrs. Dingle would notice in a moment.

"Princess—" he said, in a horrified whisper, "Princess—"

Slowly the tenseness of her body relaxed, her eyes veiled again, she grew calm.

"Yes, Tommy?" she said, in her usual voice, but there was still something about her...

"Nothing, only—oh, hang—he's starting!" said Tommy, as M. Tibault, his hands loosely clasped before him, turned and faced the audience. His eyes dropped, his tail switched once impressively, then gave three little preliminary taps with his baton on the floor.

Seldom has Gluck's overture to "Iphigenie in Aulis" received such an ovation. But it was not until the Eighth Symphony that the hysteria of the audience reached its climax. Never before had the New Symphony played so superbly—and certainly never before had it been led with such genius. Three prominent conductors in the audience were sobbing with the despairing admiration of envious children toward the close, and one at least was heard to offer wildly ten thousand dollars to a well-known facial surgeon there present for a shred of evidence that tails of some variety could by any stretch of science be grafted upon a normally decaudate form. There was no doubt about it—no mortal hand and arm, be they ever so dexterous, could combine the delicate élan and powerful grace displayed in every gesture of M. Tibault's tail.

A sable staff, it dominated the brasses like a flicker of black lightning; an ebon, elusive whip, it drew the last exquisite breath of melody from the woodwinds and ruled the stormy strings like a magician's rod. M. Tibault bowed and bowed again—roar after roar of frenzied admiration shook the hall to its foundations—and when he finally staggered, exhausted, from the platform, the president of the Wednesday Sonata Club was only restrained by force from flinging her ninety-thousand-dollar string of pearls after him in an excess of aesthetic appreciation. New York had come and seen—and New York was conquered. Mrs. Dingle was immediately besieged by reporters, and Tommy Brooks looked forward to the "little party" at which he was to meet the new hero of the hour with feelings only a little less lugubrious than those that would have come to him just before taking his seat in the electric chair.

The meeting between his Princess and M. Tibault was worse and better than he expected. Better because, after all, they did not say much to each other—and worse because it seemed to him, somehow, that some curious kinship of mind between them made words unnecessary. They were certainly the most distinguished—looking couple in the room, as he bent over her hand. "So darlingly foreign, both of them, and yet so different," babbled Mrs. Dingle—but Tommy couldn't agree.

They were different, yes—the dark, lithe stranger with the bizarre appendage tucked carelessly in his pocket, and the blue-eyed, brown-haired girl. But that difference only accentuated what they had in common—something in the way they moved, in the suavity of their gestures, in the set of their eyes. Something deeper, even, than race. He tried to puzzle it out—then, looking around at the others, he had a flash of revelation. It was as if that couple were foreign, indeed—not only to New York but to all common humanity. As if they were polite guests from a different star.

Tommy did not have a very happy evening, on the whole. But his mind worked slowly, and it was not until much later that the mad suspicion came upon him in full force.

Perhaps he is not to be blamed for his lack of immediate comprehension. The next few weeks were weeks of bewildered misery for him. It was not that the Princess's attitude toward him had changed—she was just as tolerant of him as before, but M. Tibault was always there. He had a faculty of appearing as out of thin air—he walked, for all his height, as lightly as a butterfly—and Tommy grew to hate that faintest shuffle on the carpet that announced his presence.

And then, hang it all, the man was so smooth, so infernally, unrufflably smooth! He was never out of temper, never embarrassed. He treated Tommy with the extreme of urbanity, and yet his eyes mocked, deep-down, and Tommy could do nothing. And, gradually, the Princess became more and more drawn to this stranger, in a soundless communion that found little need for speech—and that, too, Tommy saw and hated, and that, too, he could not mend.

He began to be haunted not only by M. Tibault in the flesh, but by M. Tibault in the spirit. He slept badly, and when he slept, he dreamed of—M. Tibault, a man no longer, but a shadow, a spectre, the limber ghost of an animal whose words came purringly between sharp little pointed teeth. There was certainly something odd about the whole shape of the fellow—his fluid ease, the mould of his head, even the cut of his fingernails—but just what it was escaped Tommy's intensest cogitation. And when he did put his finger on it at length, at first he refused to believe.

A pair of petty incidents decided him, finally, against all reason. He had gone to Mrs. Dingle's, one winter afternoon, hoping to find the Princess. She was out with his aunt, but was expected back for tea, and he wandered idly into the library to wait. He was just about to switch on the lights, for the library was always dark even in summer, when he heard a sound of light breathing that seemed to come from the leather couch in the corner. He approached it cautiously and dimly made out the form of M. Tibault, curled up on the couch, peacefully asleep.

The sight annoyed Tommy so that he swore under his breath and was back near the door on his way out, when the feeling we all know and hate, the feeling that eyes we cannot see are watching us, arrested him. He turned back—M. Tibault had not moved a muscle of his body to all appearance but his eyes were open now. And those eyes were black and human no longer. They were green—Tommy could have sworn it—and he could have sworn that they had no bottom and gleamed like little emeralds in the dark. It only lasted a moment, for Tommy pressed the light-button automatically—and there was M. Tibault, his normal self, yawning a little but urbanely apologetic, but it gave Tommy time to think. Nor did what happened a trifle later increase his peace of mind.

They had lit a fire and were talking in front of it—by now Tommy hated M. Tibault so thoroughly that he felt that odd yearning for his company that often occurs in such cases. M. Tibault was telling some anecdote and Tommy was hating him worse than ever for basking with such obvious enjoyment in the heat of the flames and the ripple of his own voice.

Then they heard the street-door open, and M. Tibault jumped up—and jumping, caught one sock on a sharp corner of the brass fire-rail and tore it open in a jagged flap. Tommy looked down mechanically at the tear—a second's glance, but enough—for M. Tibault, for the first time in Tommy's experience, lost his temper completely. He swore violently in some spitting, foreign tongue—his face distorted suddenly—he clapped his hand over his sock. Then, glaring furiously at Tommy, he fairly sprang from the room, and Tommy could hear him scaling the stairs in long, agile bounds.

Tommy sank into a chair, careless for once of the fact that he heard the Princess's light laugh in the hall. He didn't want to see the Princess. He didn't want to see anybody. There had been something revealed when M. Tibault had torn that hole in his sock—and it was not the skin of a man. Tommy had caught a glimpse of—black plush. Black velvet. And then had come M. Tibault's sudden explosion of fury. Good *Lord*—did the man wear black velvet stockings under his ordinary socks? Or could he—could he—but here Tommy held his fevered head in his hands.

He went to Professor Tatto that evening with a series of hypothetical questions, but as he did not dare confide his real suspicions to the Professor, the hypothetical answers he received served only to confuse him the more. Then he thought of Billy Strange. Billy was a good sort, and his mind had a turn for the bizarre. Billy might be able to help.

He couldn't get hold of Billy for three days and lived through the interval in a fever of impatience. But finally they had dinner together at Billy's apartment, where his queer books were, and Tommy was able to blurt out the whole disordered jumble of his suspicions.

Billy listened without interrupting until Tommy was quite through. Then he pulled at his pipe. "But, my dear *man*—" he said, protestingly.

"Oh, I know—I know—" said Tommy, and waved his hands, "I know I'm crazy—you needn't tell me that—but I tell you, the man's a cat all the same no, I don't see how he could be, but he is why, hang it, in the first place, everybody knows he's got a tail!"

"Even so," said Billy, puffing. "Oh, my dear Tommy, I don't doubt you saw, or think you saw, everything you say. But, even so—" He shook his head.

"But what about those other birds, werwolves and things?" said Tommy.

Billy looked dubious. "We-11," he admitted, "you've got me there, of course. At least—a tailed man *is* possible. And the yarns about werwolves go back far enough, so that—well, I wouldn't say there aren't or haven't been werwolves—but then I'm willing to believe more things than most people. But a wer-cat or a man that's a cat and a cat that's a man—honestly, Tommy—"

"If I don't get some real advice I'll go clean off my hinge. For Heaven's sake, tell me something to *do!*"

"Lemme think," said Billy. "First, you're pizen-sure this man is—"

"A cat. Yeah," and Tommy nodded violently.

"Check. And second if it doesn't hurt your feelings, Tommy you're afraid this girl you're in love with has—er—at least a streak of—felinity—in her and so she's drawn to him?"

"Oh, Lord, Billy, if I only knew!"

"Well—er—suppose she really is, too, you know—would you still be keen on her?"

"I'd marry her if she turned into a dragon every Wednesday!" said Tommy, fervently.

Billy smiled. "H'm," he said, "then the obvious thing to do is to get rid of this M. Tibault. Lemme think."

He thought about two pipes full, while Tommy sat on pins and needles. Then, finally, he burst out laughing.

"What's so darn funny?" said Tommy, aggrievedly.

"Nothing, Tommy, only I've just thought of a stunt some—thing so blooming crazy—but if he is—h'm—what you think he is—it might work—" And, going to the bookcase, he took down a book.

"If you think you're going to quiet my nerves by reading me a bedtime story—"

"Shut up, Tommy, and listen to this if you really want to get rid of your feline friend."

"What is it?"

"Book of Agnes Repplier's. About cats. Listen.

"'There is also a Scandinavian version of the ever famous story which Sir Walter Scott told to Washington Irving, which Monk Lewis told to Shelley and which, in one form or another, we find embodied in the folklore of every land'—now, Tommy, pay attention—'the story of the traveller who saw within a ruined abbey, a procession of cats, lowering into a grave a little coffin with a crown upon it. Filled with horror, he hastened from the spot; but when he had reached his destination, he could not forbear relating to a friend the wonder he had seen. Scarcely had the tale been told when his friend's cat, who lay curled up tranquilly by the fire, sprang to its feet, cried out, "Then I am the King of the Cats!" and disappeared in a flash up the chimney.'

"Well?" said Billy, shutting the book.

"By gum!" said Tommy, staring. "By gum! Do you think there's a chance?"

"*I* think we're both in the booby-hatch. But if you want to try it—"

"Try it! I'll spring it on him the next time I see him. But—listen—I can't make it a ruined abbey—"

"Oh, use your imagination! Make it Central Park—anywhere. Tell it as if it happened to you seeing the funeral procession and all that. You can lead into it somehow—let's see—some general line oh, yes— 'Strange, isn't it, how fact so often copies fiction. Why, only yesterday—' See?"

"Strange, isn't it, how fact so often copies fiction," repeated Tommy dutifully. "Why, only yesterday—"

"I happened to be strolling through Central Park when I saw something very odd."

"I happened to be strolling through—here, gimme that book!" said Tommy, "I want to learn the rest of it by heart! "

Mrs. Dingle's farewell dinner to the famous Monsieur Tibault, on the occasion of his departure for his Western tour, was looked forward to with the greatest expectations. Not only would everybody be there, including the Princess Vivrakanarda, but Mrs. Dingle, a hinter if there ever was one, had let it be known that at this dinner an announcement of very unusual interest to Society might be made. So everyone, for once, was almost on time, except for Tommy. He was at least fifteen minutes early, for he wanted to have speech with his aunt alone. Unfortunately, however, he had hardly taken off his overcoat when she was whispering some news in his ear so rapidly that he found it difficult to understand a word of it.

"And you mustn't breathe it to a soul!" she ended, beaming. "That is, not before the announcement—I think we'll have that with the salad—people never pay very much attention to salad—"

"Breathe what, Aunt Emily?" said Tommy, confused.

"The Princess, darling the dear Princess and Monsieur Tibault—they just got engaged this afternoon, dear things! Isn't it *fascinating?*"

"Yeah," said Tommy, and started to walk blindly through the nearest door. His aunt restrained him.

"Not there, dear—not in the library. You can congratulate them later. They're just having a sweet little moment alone there now—" And she turned away to harry the butler, leaving Tommy stunned.

But his chin came up after a moment. He wasn't beaten yet.

"Strange, isn't it, how often fact copies fiction?" he repeated to himself in dull mnemonics, and, as he did so, he shook his fist at the library door.

Mrs. Dingle was wrong, as usual. The Princess and M. Tibault were not in the library—they were in the conservatory, as Tommy discovered when he wandered aimlessly past the glass doors.

He didn't mean to look, and after a second he turned away. But that second was enough.

Tibault was seated in a chair and she was crouched on a stool at his side, while his hand, softly, smoothly, stroked her brown hair. Black cat and Siamese kitten. Her face was hidden from Tommy, but he could see Tibault's face. And he could hear.

They were not talking, but there was a sound between them. A warm and contented sound like the murmur of giant bees in a hollow tree—a golden, musical rumble, deep-throated, that came from Tibault's lips and was answered by hers—a golden purr.

Tommy found himself back in the drawing-room, shaking hands with Mrs. Culverin, who said, frankly, that she had seldom seen him look so pale.

The first two courses of the dinner passed Tommy like dreams, but Mrs. Dingle's cellar was notable, and by the middle of the meat course, he began to come to himself. He had only one resolve now.

For the next few moments he tried desperately to break into the conversation, but Mrs. Dingle was talking, and even Gabriel will have a time interrupting Mrs. Dingle. At last, though, she paused for breath and Tommy saw his chance.

"Speaking of that," said Tommy, piercingly, without knowing in the least what he was referring to, "Speaking of that—"

"As I was saying," said Professor Tatto. But Tommy would not yield. The plates were being taken away. It was time for salad.

"Speaking of that," he said again, so loudly and strangely that Mrs. Culverin jumped and an awkward hush fell over the table. "Strange, isn't it, how often fact copies fiction?" There, he was started. His voice rose even higher. "Why, only today I was strolling through—" and, word for word, he repeated his lesson. He could see Tibault's eyes glowing at him, as he described the funeral. He could see the Princess, tense.

He could not have said what he had expected might happen

when he came to the end; but it was not bored silence, everywhere, to be followed by Mrs. Dingle's acrid, "Well, Tommy, is that *quite* all?"

He slumped back in his chair, sick at heart. He was a fool and his last resource had failed. Dimly he heard his aunt's voice, saying, " Well, then—" and realized that she was about to make the fatal announcement.

But just then Monsieur Tibault spoke.

"One moment, Mrs. Dingle," he said, with extreme politeness, and she was silent. He turned to Tommy.

"You are—positive, I suppose, of what you saw this afternoon, Brooks?" he said, in tones of light mockery.

"Absolutely," said Tommy sullenly. "Do you think I'd—"

"Oh, no, no, no," Monsieur Tibault waved the implication aside, "but—such an interesting story—one likes to be sure of the details and, of course, you *are* sure—*quite* sure that the kind of crown you describe was on the coffin?"

"Of course," said Tommy, wondering, "but—"

"Then I'm the King of the Cats!" cried Monsieur Tibault in a voice of thunder, and, even as he cried it, the house-lights blinked—there was the soft thud of an explosion that seemed muffled in cotton-wool from the minstrel gallery—and the scene was lit for a second by an obliterating and painful burst of light that vanished in an instant and was succeeded by heavy, blinding clouds of white, pungent smoke.

"Oh, those *horrid* photographers," came Mrs. Dingle's voice in a melodious wail. "I *told* them not to take the flashlight picture till dinner was over, and now they've taken it *just* as I was nibbling lettuce!"

Someone tittered a little nervously. Someone coughed. Then, gradually the veils of smoke dislimned and the green-and-black spots in front of Tommy's eyes died away.

They were blinking at each other like people who have just come out of a cave into brilliant sun. Even yet their eyes stung with the fierceness of that abrupt illumination and Tommy found it hard to make out the faces across the table from him.

Mrs. Dingle took command of the half-blinded company with her accustomed poise. She rose, glass in hand. "And now, dear friends," she said in a clear voice, "I'm sure all of us are very happy to—" Then she stopped, open-mouthed, an expression of incredulous horror on her features. The lifted glass began to spill its contents on the tablecloth in a little stream of amber. As she spoke, she had turned directly to Monsieur Tibault's place at the table—and Monsieur Tibault was no longer there.

Some say there was a bursting flash of fire that disappeared up the chimney—some say it was a giant cat that leaped through the window at a bound, without breaking the glass. Professor Tatto puts it down to a mysterious chemical disturbance operating only over M. Tibault's chair. The butler, who is pious, believes the devil in person flew away with him, and Mrs. Dingle hesitates between witchcraft and a malicious ectoplasm dematerializing on the wrong cosmic plane. But be that as it may, one thing is certain—in the instant of fictive darkness which followed the glare of the flashlight, Monsieur Tibault, the great conductor, disappeared forever from mortal sight, tail and all.

Mrs. Culverin swears he was an international burglar and that she was just about to unmask him, when he slipped away under cover of the flashlight smoke, but no one else who sat at that historic dinner-table believes her. No, there are no sound explanations, but Tommy thinks he knows, and he will never be able to pass a cat again without wondering.

Mrs. Tommy is quite of her husband's mind regarding cats—she was Gretchen Woolwine, of Chicago—for Tommy told her his whole story, and while she doesn't believe a great deal of it, there is no doubt in her heart that one person concerned in the affair was a *perfect* cat. Doubtless it would have been more romantic to relate how Tommy's daring finally won him his Princess—but, unfortunately, it would not be veracious. For the Princess Vivrakanarda, also, is with us no longer. Her nerves, shattered by the spectacular denouement of Mrs. Dingle's dinner, required a sea-voyage, and from that voyage she has never returned to America.

Of course, there are the usual stories—one hears of her, a nun in a Siamese convent, or a masked dancer at Le Jardin de ma Soeur—one hears that she has been murdered in Patagonia or married in Trebizond—but, as far as can be ascertained, not one of these gaudy fables has the slightest basis of fact. I believe that Tommy, in his heart of hearts, is quite convinced that the sea-voyage was only a pretext, and that by some unheard-of means, she has managed to rejoin the formidable Monsieur Tibault, wherever in the world of the visible or the invisible he may be—in fact, that in some ruined city or subterranean palace they reign together now, King and Queen of all the mysterious Kingdom of Cats. But that, or course, is quite impossible.

Doc Mellhorn and the Pearly Gates
(1938)

Doc Mellhorn had never expected to go anywhere at all when he died. So, when he found himself on the road again, it surprised him. But perhaps I'd better explain a little about Doc Mellhorn first. He was seventy-odd when he left our town; but when he came, he was as young as Bates or Filsinger or any of the boys at the hospital. Only there wasn't any hospital when he came. He came with a young man's beard and a brand-new bag and a lot of newfangled ideas about medicine that we didn't take to much. And he left, forty-odd years later, with a first-class county health record and a lot of people alive that wouldn't have been alive if he hadn't been there. Yes, a country doctor. And nobody ever called him a man in white or a death grappler that I know of, though they did think of giving him a degree at Pewauket College once. But then the board met again and decided they needed a new gymnasium, so they gave the degree to J. Prentiss Parmalee instead.

They say he was a thin young man when he first came, a thin young man with an Eastern accent who'd wanted to study in Vienna. But most of us remember him chunky and solid, with white hair and a little bald spot that always got burned bright red in the first hot weather. He had about four card tricks that he'd do for you, if you were a youngster—they were always the same ones—and now and then, if he felt like it, he'd take a silver half dollar out of the back of your neck. And that worked as well with the youngsters who were going to build rocket ships as it had with the youngsters who were going to be railway engineers. It always worked. I guess it was Doc Mellhorn more than the trick.

But there wasn't anything unusual about him, except maybe the card tricks. Or, anyway, he didn't think so. He was just a good doctor and he knew us inside out. I've heard people call him a pigheaded, obstinate old mule that was in the fight about the water supply. And I've heard a weepy old lady call him a saint. I took the tale to him once, and he looked at me over his glasses and said, "Well, I've always respected a mule. Got ten times the sense of a—horse." Then he took a silver half dollar out of my ear.

Well, how do you describe a man like that? You don't—you call him up at three in the morning. And when he sends in his bill, you think it's a little steep.

All the same, when it came to it, there were people who drove a hundred and fifty miles to the funeral. And the Masons came down from Bluff City, and the Poles came from across the tracks, with a wreath the size of a house, and you saw cars in town that you didn't often see there. But it was after the funeral that the queer things began for Doc Mellhorn.

The last thing he remembered, he'd been lying in bed, feeling pretty sick, on the whole, but glad for the rest. And now he was driving his Model T down a long straight road between rolling, misty prairies that seemed to go from nowhere to nowhere.

It didn't seem funny to him to be driving the Model T again. That was the car he'd learned on, and he kept to it till his family made him change. And it didn't seem funny to him not to be sick any more. He hadn't had much time to be sick in his life—the patients usually attended to that. He looked around for his bag, first thing, but it was there on the seat beside him. It was the old bag, not the presentation one they'd given him at the hospital, but that was all right too. It meant he was out on a call and, if he couldn't quite recollect at the moment just where the call was, it was certain to come to him. He'd wakened up often enough in his buggy, in the old days, and found the horse was taking him home, without his doing much about it. A doctor gets used to things like that.

All the same, when he'd driven and driven for some time without raising so much as a traffic light, just the same rolling prairies on either hand, he began to get a little suspicious. He thought, for a while, of stopping the car and getting out, just to take a look around, but he'd always hated to lose time on a call. Then he noticed something else. He was driving without his glasses. And yet he hadn't driven without his glasses in fifteen years.

"H'm," said Doc Mellhorn. "I'm crazy as a June bug. Or else—Well, it might be so, I suppose."

But this time he did stop the car. He opened his bag and looked inside it, but everything seemed to be in order. He opened his wallet and looked at that, but there were his own initials, half rubbed away, and he recognized them. He took his pulse, but it felt perfectly steady.

"H'm," said Doc Mellhorn. "Well."

Then, just to prove that everything was perfectly normal, he took a silver half dollar out of the steering wheel of the car.

"Never did it smoother," said Doc Mellhorn. "Well, all the same, if this is the new highway, it's longer than I remember it."

But just then a motorcycle came roaring down the road and stopped with a flourish, the way motor cops do.

"Any trouble?" said the motor cop. Doc Mellhorn couldn't

see his face for his goggles, but the goggles looked normal.

"I am a physician," said Doc Mellhorn, as he'd said a thousand times before to all sorts of people, "on my way to an urgent case." He passed his hand across his forehead. "Is this the right road?" he said.

"Straight ahead to the traffic light," said the cop. "They're expecting you, Doctor Mellhorn. Shall I give you an escort?"

"No; thanks all the same," said Doc Mellhorn, and the motor cop roared away. The Model T ground as Doc Mellhorn gassed her. "Well, they've got a new breed of traffic cop," said Doc Mellhorn, "or else—"

But when he got to the light, it was just like any light at a crossroads. He waited till it changed and the officer waved him on. There seemed to be a good deal of traffic going the other way, but he didn't get a chance to notice it much, because Lizzie bucked a little, as she usually did when you kept her waiting. Still, the sight of traffic relieved him, though he hadn't passed anybody on his own road yet.

Pretty soon he noticed the look of the country had changed. It was parkway now and very nicely landscaped. There was dogwood in bloom on the little hills, white and pink against the green; though, as Doc Mellhorn remembered it, it had been August when he left his house. And every now and then there'd be a nice little white-painted sign that said TO THE GATES.

"H'm," said Doc Mellhorn. "New State Parkway, I guess. Well, they've fixed it up pretty. But I wonder where they got the dogwood. Haven't seen it bloom like that since I was East."

Then he drove along in a sort of dream for a while, for the dogwood reminded him of the days when he was a young man in an Eastern college. He remembered the look of that college and the girls who'd come to dances, the girls who wore white gloves and had rolls of hair. They were pretty girls, too, and he wondered what had become of them. "Had babies, I guess," thought Doc Mellhorn. "Or some of them, anyway." But he liked to think of them as the way they had been when they were just pretty, and excited at being at a dance.

He remembered other things too—the hacked desks in the lecture rooms, and the trees on the campus, and the first pipe he'd ever broken in, and a fellow called Paisley Grew that he hadn't thought of in years—a rawboned fellow with a gift for tall stories and playing the jew's-harp.

"Ought to have looked up Paisley," he said. "Yes, I ought. Didn't amount to a hill of beans, I guess, but I always liked him. I wonder if he still plays the jew's-harp. Pshaw, I know he's been dead twenty years."

He was passing other cars now and other cars were passing him, but he didn't pay much attention, except when he happened to notice a license you didn't often see in the state, like Rhode Island or Mississippi. He was too full of his own thoughts. There were foot passengers, too, plenty of them—and once he passed a man driving a load of hay. He wondered what the man would do with the hay when he got to the Gates. But probably there were arrangements for that.

"Not that I believe a word of it," he said, "but it'll surprise Father Kelly. Or maybe it won't. I used to have some handsome arguments with that man, but I always knew I could count on him, in spite of me being a heretic."

Then he saw the Wall and the Gates, right across the valley. He saw them, and they reached to the top of the sky. He rubbed his eyes for a while, but they kept on being there.

"Quite a sight," said Doc Mellhorn.

No one told him just where to go or how to act, but it seemed to him that he knew. If he'd thought about it, he'd have said that you waited in line, but there wasn't any waiting in line. He just went where he was expected to go and the reception clerk knew his name right away.

"Yes, Doctor Mellhorn," he said. "And now, what would you like to do first?"

"I think I'd like to sit down," said Doc Mellhorn. So he sat, and it was a comfortable chair. He even bounced the springs of it once or twice, till he caught the reception clerk's eye on him.

"Is there anything I can get you?" said the reception clerk. He was young and brisk and neat as a pin, and you could see he aimed to give service and studied about it. Doc Mellhorn thought, "He's the kind that wipes off your windshield no matter how clean it is.

"No," said Doc Mellhorn. "You see, I don't believe this. I don't believe any of it. I'm sorry if that sounds cranky, but I don't."

"That's quite all right, sir," said the reception clerk. "It often takes a while." And he smiled as if Doc Mellhorn had done him a favor.

"Young man, I'm a physician," said Doc Mellhorn, "and do you mean to tell me—"

Then he stopped, for he suddenly saw there was no use arguing. He was either there or he wasn't. And it felt as if he were there.

"Well," said Doc Mellhorn, with a sigh, "how do I begin?"

"That's entirely at your own volition, sir," said the reception clerk briskly. "Any meetings with relatives, of course. Or if you would prefer to get yourself settled first. Or take a tour, alone or conducted. Perhaps these will offer suggestions," and he started to hand over a handful of leaflets. But Doc Mellhorn put them aside.

"Wait a minute," he said. "I want to think. Well, naturally, there's Mother and Dad. But I couldn't see them just yet. I wouldn't believe it. And Grandma—well, now, if I saw Grandma and me older than she is—was—used to be—well, I don't know—what it would do to me. You've got to let me get my breath. Well, of course, there's Uncle Frank—he'd be easier." He paused. "Is he here?" he said.

The reception clerk looked in a file. "I am happy to say that Mr. Francis V. Mellhorn arrived July 12, 1907," he said. He smiled winningly.

"Well!" said Doc Mellhorn. "Uncle Frank! Well, I'll be—well! But it must have been a great consolation to Mother. We heard—well, never mind what we heard—I guess it wasn't so.... No, don't reach for that phone just yet, or whatever it is. I'm still thinking."

"We sometimes find," said the reception clerk eagerly, "that a person not a relative may be the best introduction. Even a stranger sometimes a distinguished stranger connected with one's own profession—"

"Well, now, that's an idea," said Doc Mellhorn heartily, trying to keep his mind off how much he disliked the reception clerk. He couldn't just say why he disliked him, but he knew he did.

It reminded him of the time he'd had to have his gall bladder out in the city hospital and the young, brisk interns had come to see him and called him "Doctor" every other word.

"Yes, that's an idea," he said. He reflected. "Well, of course, I'd like to see Koch," he said. "And Semmelweiss, Not to speak of Walter Reed. But, shucks, they'd be busy men. But there is one fellow—only he lived pretty far back—"

"Hippocrates, please," said the reception clerk into the telephone or whatever it was. "*H* for horse—"

"No!" said Doc Mellhorn quite violently. "Excuse me, but you just wait a minute. I mean if you can wait. I mean, if Hippocrates wants to come, I've no objection. But I never took much of a fancy to him, in spite of his oath. It's Aesculapius I'm thinking about. George W. Oh, glory!" he said. "But he won't talk English. I forgot."

"I shall be happy to act as interpreter," said the reception clerk, smiling brilliantly.

"I haven't a doubt," said Doc Mellhorn. "But just wait a shake." In a minute, by the way the clerk was acting, he was going to be talking to Aesculapius. "And what in time am I going to say to the man?" he thought. "It's too much." He gazed wildly around the neat reception room—distempered, as he noticed, in a warm shade of golden tan. Then his eyes fell on the worn black bag at his feet and a sudden warm wave of relief flooded over him.

"Wait a minute," he said, and his voice gathered force and authority. "Where's my patient?"

"Patient?" said the reception clerk, looking puzzled for the first time.

"Patient," said Doc Mellhorn. "P for phlebitis." He tapped his bag.

"I'm afraid you don't quite understand, sir," said the reception clerk.

"I understand this," said Doc Mellhorn. "I was called here. And if I wasn't called professionally, why have I got my bag?"

"But, my dear Doctor Mellhorn—" said the reception clerk.

"I'm not your dear doctor," said Doc Mellhorn. "I was called here, I tell you. I'm sorry not to give you the patient's name, but the call must have come in my absence and the girl doesn't spell very well. But in any well-regulated hospital—"

"But I tell you," said the reception clerk, and his hair wasn't slick any more, "nobody's ill here. Nobody can be ill. If they could, it wouldn't be He—"

"Humph," said Doc Mellhorn. He thought it over, and felt worse. "Then what does a fellow like Koch do?" he said. "Or Pasteur?" He raised a hand. "Oh, don't tell me," he said. "I can see they'd be busy. Yes, I guess it'd be all right for a research man. But I never was... Oh, well, shucks, I've published a few papers. And there's that clamp of mine—always meant to do something about it. But they've got better ones now. Mean to say there isn't so much as a case of mumps in the whole place?"

"I assure you," said the reception clerk, in a weary voice. "And now, once you see Doctor Aesculapius—"

"Funny," said Doc Mellhorn. "Lord knows there's plenty of times you'd be glad to be quit of the whole thing. And don't talk to me about the healer's art or grateful patients. Well, I've known a few... a few. But I've known others. All the same, it's different, being told there isn't any need for what you can do."

"*A* for Ararat," said the reception clerk into his instrument. "*E* for Eden."

"Should think you'd have a dial," said Doc Mellhorn desperately. "We've got 'em down below." He thought hard and frantically. "Wait a shake. It's coming back to me," he said. "Got anybody named Grew here? Paisley Grew?"

"*S* for serpent..." said the reception clerk. "What was that?"

"Fellow that called me," said Doc Mellhorn. "G-r-e-w. First name, Paisley."

"I will consult the index," said the reception clerk.

He did so, and Doc Mellhorn waited, hoping against hope.

"We have 94,183 Grews, including 83 Prescotts and one Penobscot," the reception clerk said at last. "But I fail to find Paisley Grew. Are you quite sure of the name?"

"Of course," said Doc Mellhorn briskly. "Paisley Grew. Chronic indigestion. Might be appendix—can't say—have to see. But anyhow, he's called." He picked up his bag. "Well, thanks for the information," he said, liking the reception clerk better than he had yet. "Not your fault, anyway."

"But—but where are you going?" said the reception clerk.

"Well, there's another establishment, isn't there?" said Doc Mellhorn. "Always heard there was. Call probably came from there. Crossed wires, I expect."

"But you can't go there!" said the reception clerk. "I mean—"

"Can't go?" said Doc Mellhorn. "I'm a physician. A patient's called me."

"But if you'll only wait and sec Aesculapius!" said the reception clerk, running his hands wildly through his hair. "He'll be here almost any moment."

"Please give him my apologies," said Doc Mellhorn. "He's a doctor. He'll understand. And if any messages come for me, just stick them on the spike. Do I need a road map? Noticed the road I came was all one way."

"There is, I believe, a back road in rather bad repair," said the reception clerk icily. "I can call Information if you wish."

"Oh, don't bother," said Doc Mellhorn. "I'll find it. And I never saw a road beat Lizzie yet." He took a silver half dollar from the doorknob of the door. "See that?" he said. "Slick as a whistle. Well, good-by, young man."

But it wasn't till he'd cranked up Lizzie and was on his way that Doc Mellhorn really felt safe. He found the back road and it was all the reception clerk had said it was and more. But he didn't mind—in fact, after one particularly bad rut, he grinned.

"I suppose I ought to have seen the folks," he said. "Yes, I know I ought. But—not so much as a case of mumps in the whole abiding dominion! Well, it's lucky I took a chance on Paisley Grew."

After another mile or so, he grinned again.

"And I'd like to see old Aesculapius' face. Probably rang him in the middle of dinner—they always do. But shucks, it's happened to all of us."

Well, the road got worse and worse and the sky above it darker and darker, and what with one thing and another, Doc Mellhorn was glad enough when he got to the other gates. They were pretty impressive gates, too, though of course in a different way, and reminded Doc Mellhorn a little of the furnaces outside Steeltown, where he'd practiced for a year when he was young.

This time Doc Mellhorn wasn't going to take any advice from reception clerks and he had his story all ready. All the same, he wasn't either registered or expected, so there was a little fuss. Finally they tried to scare him by saying he came at his own risk and that there were some pretty tough characters about. But Doc Mellhorn remarked that he'd practiced in Steeltown. So, after he'd told them what seemed to him a million times that he was a physician on a case, they finally let him in and directed him to Paisley Grew. Paisley was on Level 346 in Pit 68,953, andDoc Mellhorn recognized him the minute he saw him. He even had the jew's-harp, stuck in the back of his overalls.

"Well, Doc," said Paisley finally, when the first greetings were over, "you certainly are a sight for sore eyes! Though, of course, I'm sorry to see you here," and he grinned.

"Well, I can't see that it's so different from a lot of places," said Doc Mellhorn, wiping his forehead. "Warmish, though."

"It's the humidity, really," said Paisley Grew. "That's what it really is."

"Yes, I know," said Doc Mellhorn. "And now tell me, Paisley; how's that indigestion of yours?"

"Well, I'll tell you, Doc," said Paisley. "When I first came here, I thought the climate was doing it good. I did for a fact. But now I'm not so sure. I've tried all sorts of things for it—I've even tried being transferred to the boiling asphalt lakes. But it just seems to hang on, and every now and then, when I least expect it, it catches me. Take last night. I didn't have a thing to eat that I don't generally eat—well, maybe I did have one little snort of hot sulphur, but it wasn't the sulphur that did it. All the same, I woke up at four, and it was just like a knife. Now…"

He went on from there and it took him some time. And Doc Mellhorn listened, happy as a clam. He never thought he'd be glad to listen to a hypochondriac, but he was. And when Paisley was all through, he examined him and prescribed for him. It was just a little soda bicarb and pepsin, but Paisley said it took hold something wonderful. And they had a fine time that evening, talking over the old days.

Finally, of course, the talk got around to how Paisley liked it where he was. And Paisley was honest enough about that.

"Well, Doc," he said, "of course this isn't the place for you, and I can see you're just visiting. But I haven't many real complaints. It's hot, to be sure, and they work you, and some of the boys here are rough. But they've had some pretty interesting experiences, too, when you get them talking—yes, sir. And anyhow, it isn't Peabodyville, New Jersey," he said with vehemence. "I spent five years in Peabodyville, trying to work up in the leather business. After that I bust out, and I guess that's what landed me here. But it's an improvement on Peabodyville." He looked at Doc Mellhorn sidewise. "Say, Doc," he said, "I know this is a vacation for you, but all the same there's a couple of the boys—nothing really wrong with them of course—but—well, if you could just look them over—"

"I was thinking the office hours would be nine to one," said Doc Mellhorn.

So Paisley took him around and they found a nice little place for an office in one of the abandoned mine galleries, and Doc

Mellhorn hung out his shingle. And right away patients started coming around. They didn't get many doctors there, in the first place, and the ones they did get weren't exactly the cream of the profession, so Doc Mellhorn had it all to himself. It was mostly sprains, fractures, bruises and dislocations, of course, with occasional burns and scalds—and, on the whole, it reminded Doc Mellhorn a good deal of his practice in Steeltown, especially when it came to foreign bodies in the eye. Now and then Doc Mellhorn ran into a more unusual case—for instance, there was one of the guards that got part of himself pretty badly damaged in a rock slide. Well, Doc Mellhorn had never set a tail before, but he managed it all right, and got a beautiful primary union, too, in spite of the fact that he had no X-ray facilities. He thought of writing up the case for the State Medical Journal, but then he couldn't figure out any way to send it to them, so he had to let it slide. And then there was an advanced carcinoma of the liver—a Greek named Papadoupolous or Prometheus or something. Doc Mellhorn couldn't do much for him, considering the circumstances, but he did what he could, and he and the Greek used to have long conversations. The rest was just everyday practice—run of the mine—but he enjoyed it.

Now and then it would cross his mind that he ought to get out Lizzie and run back to the other place for a visit with the folks. But that was just like going back East had been on earth—he'd think he had everything pretty well cleared up, and then a new flock of patients would come in. And it wasn't that he didn't miss his wife and children and grandchildren—he did. But there wasn't any way to get back to them, and he knew it. And there was the work in front of him and the office crowded every day. So he just went along, hardly noticing the time.

Now and then, to be sure, he'd get a suspicion that he wasn't too popular with the authorities of the place. But he was used to not being popular with authorities and he didn't pay much attention. But finally they sent an inspector around. The minute Doc Mellhorn saw him, he knew there was going to be trouble.

Not that the inspector was uncivil. In fact, he was a pretty high-up official—you could tell by his antlers. And Doc Mellhorn was just as polite, showing him around. He showed him the free dispensary and the clinic and the nurse—Scotch girl named Smith, she was—and the dental chair he'd rigged up with the help of a fellow named Ferguson, who used to be an engineer before he was sentenced. And the inspector looked them all over, and finally he came back to Doc Mellhorn's office. The girl named Smith had put up curtains in the office, and with that and a couple of potted gas plants it looked more homelike than it had. The inspector looked around it and sighed.

"I'm sorry, Doctor Mellhorn," he said at last, "but you can see for yourself, it won't do."

"What won't do?" said Doc Mellhorn, stoutly. But, all the same, he felt afraid.

"Any of it," said the inspector. "We could overlook the alleviation of minor suffering—I d be inclined to do so myself—though these people are here to suffer, and there's no changing that. But you're playing merry Hades with the whole system."

"I'm a physician in practice," said Doc Mellhorn.

"Yes," said the inspector. "That's just the trouble. New, take these reports you've been sending," and he took out a sheaf of papers. "What have you to say about that?"

Well, seeing as there's no county health officer, or at least I couldn't find one—" said Doc Mellhorn.

"Precisely," said the inspector. "And what have you done? You've condemned fourteen levels of this pit as unsanitary nuisances. You've recommended 2136 lost souls for special diet, remedial exercise, hospitalization—Well—I won't go through the list."

"I'll stand back of every one of those recommendations," said Doc Mellhorn. "And now we've got the chair working, we can handle most of the dental work on the spot. Only Ferguson needs more amalgam."

"I know," said the inspector patiently, "but the money has to come from somewhere—you must realize that. We're not a rich community, in spite of what people think. And these unauthorized requests—oh, we fill them, of course, but—"

"Ferguson needs more amalgam," said Doc Mellhorn. "And that last batch wasn't standard. I wouldn't use it on a dog."

"He's always needing more amalgam!" said the inspector bitterly, making a note. "Is he going to fill every tooth in Hades? By the way, my wife tells me I need a little work done myself—but we won't go into that. We'll take just one thing—your entirely unauthorized employment of Miss Smith. Miss Smith has no business working for you. She's supposed to be gnawed by a never-dying worm every Monday, Wednesday and Friday."

"Sounds silly to me," said Doc Mellhorn.

"I don't care how silly it sounds," said the inspector. "It's regulations. And, besides, she isn't even a registered nurse."

"She's a practical one," said Doc Mellhorn. "Of course, back on earth a lot of her patients died. But that was because when she didn't like a patient, she poisoned him. Well, she can't poison anybody here and I've kind of got her out of the notion of it anyway. She's been doing A-1 work for me and I'd like to recommend her for—"

"Please!" said the inspector. "Please! And as if that wasn't enough, you've even been meddling with the staff. I've a note here on young Asmodeus—Asmodeus XIV—"

"Oh, you mean Mickey!" said Doc Mellhorn, with a chuckle.

"Short for Mickey Mouse. We call him that in the clinic. And he's a young imp if I ever saw one."

"The original Asmodeus is one of our most prominent citizens," said the inspector severely. "How do you suppose he felt when we got your report that his fourteenth great-grandson had rickets?"

"Well," said Doc Mellhorn, "I know rickets. And he had 'em. And you're going to have rickets in these youngsters as long as you keep feeding 'em low-grade coke. I put Mickey on the best Pennsylvania anthracite, and look at him now!"

"I admit the success of your treatment," said the inspector, "but, naturally—well, since then we've been deluged with demands for anthracite from as far south as Sheol. We'll have to float a new bond issue. And what will the taxpayers say?"

"He was just cutting his first horns when he came to us," said Doc Mellhorn reminiscently, "and they were coming in crooked. Now, I ask you, did you ever see a straighter pair? Of course, if I'd had cod liver oil—My gracious, you ought to have somebody here that can fill a prescription; I can't do it all."

The inspector shut his papers together with a snap. "I'm sorry, Doctor Mellhorn," he said, "but this is final. You have no right here, in the first place; no local license to practice in the second—"

"Yes, that's a little irregular," said Doc Mellhorn, "but I'm a registered member of four different medical associations—you might take that into account. And I'll take any examination that's required."

"No," said the inspector violently. "No, no, no! You can't stay here! You've got to go away! It isn't possible!"

Doc Mellhorn drew a long breath. "Well," he said, "there wasn't any work for me at the other place. And here you won't let me practice. So what's a man to do?"

The inspector was silent.

"Tell me," said Doc Mellhorn presently. "Suppose you do throw me out? What happens to Miss Smith and Paisley and the rest of them?"

"Oh, what's done is done," said the inspector impatiently, "here as well as anywhere else. We'll have to keep on with the anthracite and the rest of it. And Hades only knows what'll happen in the future. If it's any satisfaction to you, you've started something."

"Well, I guess Smith and Ferguson between them can handle the practice," said Doc Melihorn. "But that's got to be a promise."

"It's a promise," said the inspector.

"Then there's Mickey—I mean Asmodeus," said Doc Mellhorn. "He's a smart youngster—smart as a whip—if he is a hellion. Well, you know how a youngster gets. Well, it seems he wants to be a doctor. But I don't know what sort of training he'd get—"

"He'll get it," said the inspector feverishly. "We'll found the finest medical college you ever saw, right here in West Baal. We'll build a hospital that'll knock your eye out. You'll be satisfied. But now, if you don't mind—"

"All right," said Doc Mellhorn, and rose.

The inspector looked surprised. "But don't you want to—" he said. "I mean my instructions are we're to give you a banquet, if necessary—after all, the community appreciates—"

"Thanks," said Doc Mellhorn, with a shudder, "but if I've got to go, I'd rather get out of town. You hang around and announce your retirement, and pretty soon folks start thinking they ought to give you a testimonial. And I never did like testimonials."

All the same, before he left he took a silver half dollar out of Mickey Asmodeus' chin.

When he was back on the road again and the lights of the gates had faded into a low ruddy glow behind him, Doc Mellhorn felt alone for the first time. He'd been lonely at times during his life, but he'd never felt alone like this before. Because, as far as he could see, there was only him and Lizzie now.

"Now, maybe if I'd talked to Aesculapius—" he said. "But pshaw, I always was pigheaded."

He didn't pay much attention to the way he was driving and it seemed to him that the road wasn't quite the same. But he felt tired for a wonder—bone-tired and beaten—and he didn't much care about the road. He hadn't felt tired since he left earth, but now the loneliness tired him.

"Active—always been active," he said to himself. "I can't just lay down on the job. But what's a man to do?

"What's a man to do?" he said. "I'm a doctor. I can't work miracles."

Then the black fit came over him and he remembered all the times he'd been wrong and all the people he couldn't do anything for. "Never was much of a doctor, I guess," he said. "Maybe, if I'd gone to Vienna. Well, the right kind of man would have gone. And about that Bigelow kid," he said. "How was I to know he'd hemorrhage? But I should have known.

"I've diagnosed walking typhoid as appendicitis. Just the once, but that's enough. And I still don't know what held me back when I was all ready to operate. I used to wake up in a sweat, six months afterward, thinking I had.

"I could have saved those premature twins, if I'd known as much then as I do now. I guess that guy Dafoe would have done it anyway—look at what he had to work with. But I didn't. And that finished the Gorhams' having children. That's a dandy doctor, isn't it? Makes you feel fine.

"I could have pulled Old Man Halsey through. And Edna

Biggs. And the little Lauriat girl. No, I couldn't have done it with her. That was before insulin. I couldn't have cured Ted Allen. No, I'm clear on that. But I've never been satisfied about the Collins woman. Bates is all right—good as they come. But I knew her, inside and out—ought to, too—she was the biggest nuisance that ever came into the office. And if I hadn't been down with the flu...

"Then there's the flu epidemic. I didn't take my clothes off, four days and nights. But what's the good of that, when you lose them? Oh, sure, the statistics looked good. You can have the statistics.

"Should have started raising hell about the water supply two years before I did.

"Oh, yes, it makes you feel fine, pulling babies into the world. Makes you feel you're doing something. And just fine when you see a few of them, twenty-thirty years later, not worth two toots on a cow's horn. Can't say I ever delivered a Dillinger. But there's one or two in state's prison. And more that ought to be. Don't mind even that so much as a few of the fools. Makes you wonder.

"And then, there's incurable cancer. That's a daisy. What can you do about it, Doctor? Well, Doctor, we can alleviate the pain in the last stages. Some. Ever been in a cancer ward, Doctor? Yes, Doctor, I have.

"What do you do for the common cold, Doctor? Two dozen clean linen handkerchiefs. Yes, it's a good joke—I'll laugh. And what do you do for a boy when you know he's dying, Doctor? Take a silver half dollar out of his ear. But it kept the Lane kid quiet and his fever went down that night. I took the credit, but I don't know why it went down.

"I've only got one brain. And one pair of hands.

"I could have saved. I could have done. I could have.

"Guess it's just as well you can't live forever. You make fewer mistakes. And sometimes I'd see Bates looking at me as if he wondered why I ever thought I could practice.

"Pigheaded, opinionated, ineffective old imbecile! And yet, Lord, Lord, I'd do it all over again."

He lifted his eyes from the pattern of the road in front of him. There were white markers on it now and Lizzie seemed to be bouncing down a residential street. There were trees in the street and it reminded him of town. He rubbed his eyes for a second and Lizzie rolled on by herself—she often did. It didn't seem strange to him to stop at the right house.

"Well, Mother," he said rather gruffly to the group on the lawn. "Well, Dad.... Well, Uncle Frank." He beheld a small, stern figure advancing, hands outstretched. "Well, Grandma," he said meekly.

Later on he was walking up and down in the grape arbor with Uncle Frank. Now and then he picked a grape and ate it. They'd always been good grapes, those Catawbas, as he remembered them.

"What beats me," he said, not for the first time, "is why I didn't notice the Gates. The second time, I mean."

"Oh, that Gate," said Uncle Frank, with the easy, unctuous roll in his voice that Doc Mellhorn so well remembered. He smoothed his handle-bar moustaches. "That Gate, my dear Edward—well, of course it has to be there in the first place. Literature, you know. And then, it's a choice," he said richly.

"I'll draw cards," said Doc Mellhorn. He ate another grape.

"Fact is," said Uncle Frank, "that Gate's for one kind of person. You pass it and then you can rest for all eternity. Just fold your hands. It suits some."

"I can see that it would," said Doc Mellhorn.

"Yes," said Uncle Frank, "but it wouldn't suit a Mellhorn. I'm happy to say that very few of our family remain permanently on that side. I spent some time there myself." He said, rather self-consciously, "Well, my last years had been somewhat stormy. So few people cared for refined impersonations of our feathered songsters, including lightning sketches. I felt that I'd earned a rest. But after a while—well, I got tired of being at liberty."

"And what happens when you get tired?" said Doc Mellhorn.

"You find out what you want to do," said Uncle Frank.

"My kind of work?" said Doc Mellhorn.

"Your kind of work," said his uncle. "Been busy, haven't you?"

"Well," said Doc Mellhorn. "But here. If there isn't so much as a case of mumps in—"

"Would it have to be mumps?" said his uncle. "Of course, if you're aching for mumps, I guess it could be arranged. But how many new souls do you suppose we get here a day?"

"Sizable lot, I expect."

"And how many of them get here in first-class condition?" said Uncle Frank triumphantly. "Why, I've seen Doctor Rush—Benjamin Rush—come back so tired from a day's round he could hardly flap one pinion against the other. Oh, if it's work you want—And then, of course, there's the earth."

"Hold on," said Doc Mellhorn. "I'm not going to appear to any young intern in wings and a harp. Not at my time of life. And anyway, he'd laugh himself sick."

"'Tain't that," said Uncle Frank. "Look here. You've left children and grandchildren behind you, haven't you? And they're going on?"

"Yes," said Doc Mellhorn.

"Same with what you did," said Uncle Frank. "I mean the inside part of it—that stays. I don't mean any funny business—

voices in your ear and all that. But haven't you ever got clean tuckered out, and been able to draw on something you didn't know was there?"

"Pshaw, any man's done that," said Doc Mellhorn. "But you take the adrenal—"

"Take anything you like," said Uncle Frank placidly. "I'm not going to argue with you. Not my department. But you'll find it isn't all adrenalin. Like it here?" he said abruptly. "Feel satisfied?"

"Why, yes," said Doc Mellhorn surprisedly, "I do." He looked around the grape arbor and suddenly realized that he felt happy.

"No, they wouldn't all arrive in first-class, shape," he said to himself. "So there'd be a place." He turned to Uncle Frank. "By the way," he said diffidently, "I mean, I got back so quick there wouldn't be a chance of my visiting the other establishment now and then? Where I just came from? Smith and Ferguson are all right, but I'd like to keep in touch."

"Well," said Uncle Frank, "you can take that up with the delegation." He arranged the handkerchief in his breast pocket. "They ought to be along any minute now," he said. "Sister's been in a stew about it all day. She says there won't be enough chairs, but she always says that."

"Delegation?" said Doc Mellhorn. "But—"

"You don't realize," said Uncle Frank, with his rich chuckle. "You're a famous man. You've broken pretty near every regulation except the fire laws, and refused the Gate first crack. They've got to do something about it."

"But—" said Doc Mellhorn, looking wildly around for a place of escape.

"Sh-h!" hissed Uncle Frank. "Hold up your head and look as though money were bid for you. It won't take long—just a welcome." He shaded his eyes with his hand. "My," he said with frank admiration, "you've certainly brought them out. There's Rush, by the way."

"Where?" said Doc Mellhorn.

"Second from the left, third row, in a wig," said Uncle Frank. "And there's—"

Then he stopped, and stepped aside. A tall grave figure was advancing down the grape arbor—a bearded man with a wise, majestic face who wore robes as if they belonged to him, not as Doc Mellhorn had seen them worn in college commencements. There was a small fillet of gold about his head and in his left hand, Doc Mellhorn noticed without astonishment, was a winged staff entwined with two fangless serpents. Behind him were many others. Doc Mellhorn stood straighter.

The bearded figure stopped in front of Doc Mellhorn. "Welcome, Brother," said Aesculapius.

"It's an honor to meet you, Doctor," said Doc Mellhorn. He shook the outstretched hand. Then he took a silver half dollar from the mouth of the left-hand snake.

The Last of the Legions
(1937)

The governor wanted to have everything go off as quietly as possible, but he couldn't keep the people from the windows or off the streets. After all, the legion had been at Deva ever since there was a town to speak of, and now we were going away. I don't want to say anything against the Sixth or the Second—there are good men under all the eagles. But we're not called the Valeria Victrix for nothing, and we've had the name some few centuries. It takes a legion with men in it to hold the northwest.

I think, at first, they intended to keep the news secret, but how could you do that, in a town? There's always someone who tells his girl in strict confidence, and then there are all the peddlers and astrologers and riffraff, and the sharp-faced boys with tips on the races or the games. I tell you, they knew about it as soon as the general or the governor—not to speak of the rumors before. As a matter of fact, there had been so many rumors that, when the orders came at last, it was rather a relief. You get tired of telling women that nothing will happen to them even if the legion does go, and being stopped five times in ten minutes whenever you go into town.

All the same, I had to sit up half the night with one recruit of ours. He had a girl in the town he was mad about, and a crazy notion of deserting. I had to point out to the young imbecile that even if the legion goes, Rome stays, and describe the two men I'd happened to see flogged to death, before he changed his mind. The girl was a pretty little weak-mouthed thing—she was crying in the crowd when we marched by, and he bit his lips to keep steady. But I couldn't have him deserting out of our cohort—we haven't had a thing like that happen in twenty years.

It was queer, their not making more noise. They tried to cheer—governor's orders—when we turned the camp over to the native auxiliaries in the morning, but it wasn't much of a success. And yet, the auxiliaries looked well enough, for auxiliaries. I wouldn't give two cohorts of Egyptians for them myself, but they had their breastplates shined and kept a fairly straight front, I imagined they'd dirty up our quarters—auxiliaries always do—and that wasn't pleasant to think of. But the next legion that came to Deva—us or another—would put things straight again. And it couldn't be long.

Then we had our own march past—through the town—and, as I say, it was queer. I'm a child of the camp—I was brought up in the legion. The tale is that the first of us came with Caesar—I don't put much stock in that—and of course we've married British ever since. Still, I know what I know, and I know what a crowd sounds like, on most occasions. There's the mutter of a hostile one, and the shouts when they throw flowers, and the sharp, fierce cheering when they know you're going out to fight for them. But this was different. There wasn't any heart or pith in it—just a queer sort of sobbing wail that went with us all the way to the gates. Oh, here .and there, people shouted, "Come back with their heads!" or "Bring us a Goth for a pet!" the way they do, but not as if they believed what they were saying. Too many of them were silent, and that queer sort of sobbing wail went with us all the way.

I march with the first cohort; it wasn't so bad for me. Though here and there, I saw faces in the crowd—old Elfrida, who kept the wine shop, with the tears running down her fat cheeks, shouting like a good one, and Parmesius, the usurer, biting his nails and not saying anything at all. He might have given us a cheer; he'd had enough of our money. But he stood there, looking scared. I expect he was thinking of his money bags and wondering if somebody would slip a knife in his ribs at night. We'd kept good order in the town.

It took a long time, at the gates, for the governor had to make a speech—like all that old British stock, he tries to be more Roman than the Romans. Our general listened to him, sitting his horse like a bear. He's a new general, one of Stilicho's men, and a good one in spite of his hairiness and his Vandal accent. I don't think he cared very much for the governor's speech—it was the usual one. The glorious Twentieth, you know, and our gallant deeds, and how glad they'd be to have us back again. Well, we knew that without his telling—we could read it in the white faces along the walls. They were very still, but you could feel them, looking. The whole town must have been at the walls. Then the speech ended, and our general nodded his bear head and we marched. I don't know how long they stayed at the walls—I couldn't look back.

But my recruit got away, after all, at the second halt, and that bothered me. He was a likely looking young fellow, though I'd always thought his neck was too long. Still, he was one of the children of the camp—you wouldn't have picked him to desert. After that, half a dozen others tried it—those things are like a disease—but our general caught two and made an example, and that stopped the rest. I don't care for torture, myself—it leaves a bad taste in your mouth but there are times when you have to use a firm hand. They were talking too much about Deva and remembering too many things. Well, I could see, myself, that if we had to be marched half across Britain to take ship at Anderida, that meant the Northmen were strong again. And I wouldn't like to hold the northwest against Northmen and Scots with nothing but auxiliaries. But that was the empire's business—it wasn't mine.

After it was over, I was having a cup of wine and chatting with Agathocles—he's a small man, but clever with the legion accounts and very proud that his father was a Greek. He has special privileges, and that's apt to get a man disliked, but I always got along well with him. If you're senior centurion, you have your own rights, and he didn't often try the nasty side of his tongue on me.

"Well, Death's-Head," I said—we call him that because of his bony face—"were you present at the ceremonies?"

"Oh, I was present," he said. He shivered a little. "I suppose you liked hearing them squeal," he said, with his black eyes full of malice.

"Can't say that I did," I said, "but it'll keep the recruits in order."

"For a while," he said, and laughed softly. But I wasn't really thinking of the men who had been caught—I was thinking of my own recruit who'd gotten away. I could see him, you know, quite plainly, with his long neck and his bright blue Northern eyes—a tiny, running figure, hiding in ditches and traveling by night. He'd started in full marching order, too, like an idiot. Pretty soon, he'd be throwing pieces of equipment away. And what would he do when he did get back to Deva—hide on one of the outlying farms? Our farmers were a rough lot—they'd turn him over to the governor, if they didn't cut his throat for the price of his armor. It's a bad feeling, being hunted—I've had it myself. You begin to hear noises in the bracken and feel the joints in your armor where an arrow could go through. He'd scream, too, if he were caught—scream like a hare. And all for a weak-faced girl and because he felt homesick! I couldn't understand it.

"Worried about your recruit?" said Agathocles, though I hadn't said a word.

"The young fool!" I said. "He should have known better."

"Perhaps he was wiser than you think," said Agathocles. "Perhaps he's a soothsayer and reads omens."

"Soothsayer!" I said. "He'll make a pretty-looking soothsayer if the governor catches him! Though I suppose he has friends in the town."

"Why, doubtless," said Agathocles. "And, after all, why should they waste a trained man? He might even change his name and join the auxiliaries. He might have a good story, you know."

I thought, for a moment. Of course they'd be slack, now we'd left, but I couldn't believe they'd be as slack as that.

"I should hope not, I'm sure," I said, rather stiffly. "After all, the man's a deserter."

"Old Faithful," said Agathocles, laughing softly. "Always Old Faithful. You like the boy, but you'd rather see him cut to ribbons like our friends today. Now, I'm a Greek and a philosopher—I look for causes and effects."

"All Greeks are eaters of wind," I said, not insultingly, you know, but just to show him where he stood. But he didn't seem to hear me.

"Yes," he said, "I look for causes and effects. You think the man a deserter, I think him a soothsayer—that is the difference between us. Would a child of the camp have deserted the legion a century ago, or two centuries ago, Old Faithful?"

"How can I tell what anyone would do a century ago?" I said, for it was a foolish question.

"Exactly," he said. "And a century ago they would not have withdrawn the Twentieth—not from that border—not unless Rome fell." He clapped me on the back with an odious familiarity. "Do not worry about your recruit, Old Faithful," he said. "Perhaps he will even go over to the other side, and, indeed, that might be wise of him."

"Talk treason to your accounts, Greek," I growled, "and take your hand off my shoulder. I am a Roman."

He looked at me with sad eyes.

"After three hundred years in Britain," he said. "And yet he says he is a Roman. Yes, it is a very strong law. And yet we had a law and states once, too, we Greeks. Be comforted, my British Roman. I am not talking treason. After all, I, too, have spent my life with the eagles. But I look for causes and effects."

He sighed in his wine cup and, in spite of his nonsense, I could not help but feel sorry for him. He was not a healthy man and his chest troubled him at night.

"Forget them," I said, "and attend to your accounts. You'll feel better when we're really on the march."

He sighed again. "Unfortunately, I am a philosopher," he said. "It takes more than exercise to cure that. I can even hear a world cracking, when it is under my nose. But you are not a philosopher, Old Faithful—do not let it give you bad dreams."

I manage to get my sleep without dreams, as a rule, so I told him that and left him. But, all the same, some of his nonsense must have stuck in my head. For, all the way down to Anderida, I kept noticing little things. Usually, on a long march, once you get into the swing of it, you live in that swing. There's the back of the neck of the man in front of you, and the weather, fine or wet, and the hairy general, riding his horse like a bear, and the dust kicked up by the column and the business of billets for the night. The town life drops away from you like a cloak you left behind in the pawnshop and, pretty soon, you've never led any other kind of life. You have to take care of your men and see the cooks are up to their work and tell from the look on a man's face whether he's the sort of fool who rubs his feet raw before he complains. And all that's pleasant enough and so is the change in the country, and the villages you go through, likely never to see again, but there was good wine in one, and a landlord's daughter in another, and perhaps you washed your feet in a third and joked with the old girl who came down by the stream and told you you were a fine-looking soldier. It's all there, and nothing to remember, but pleasant while it lasts. And, toward the end, there's the little tightness at the back of the mind that makes you know you're coming near the fighting. But, before that, you hardly think at all.

This wasn't any different and yet I kept looking at the country. I'd been south before, as far as Londinium, but not for years, and there's no denying that it's a pleasant land. A little soft, as the people are, but very green, very smiling, between the forests. You could see they took care of their fields; you could see it was a rich place, compared to the north. There were sheep in the pastures, whole flocks of them, fat and baaing, and the baths in the towns we passed through got better all the way. And yet I kept looking for places where a cohort or two could make a stand without being cut off completely—now, why should I do that? You can say it was my business, but Mid-Britain has been safe for years. You have only to look at the villas—we've got nothing like them in the northwest. I couldn't help wondering what a crew of wild Scots or long-haired Northmen would do to some of them. We'd have blocked up half those windows where I come from—once they start shooting fire arrows, big windows are a nuisance, even in a fortified town.

And yet, in spite of the way Agathocles rode along like a death's-head, it was reassuring too. For it showed you how solid the empire was, a big solid block of empire, green and smiling, with its magistrates and fine special ladies and theaters and country houses, all the way from Mid-Britain to Rome, and getting richer all the way. I didn't feel jealous about it or particularly proud, but there it was, and it meant civilized things. That's the difference between us and the barbarians—you may not think of it often, but, when you see it, you know. I remember a young boy, oh, eight or nine. He'd been sent down from the big house on his fat pony with his tutor, to look at the soldiers, and there he sat, perfectly safe, while his pony cropped the grass and the old man had a hand in the pony's mane. He was clean out of bowshot of the big house, and the hedges could have held a hundred men, but you could see he'd never been afraid in his life, or lived in disputed ground. Not even the old tutor was afraid—he must have been a slave, but he grinned at us like anything. Well, that shows you. I thought the worse of Agathocles, after that.

And yet, there were other things—oh, normal enough. But, naturally, you can't move a legion without people asking questions, and civilians are like hens when they start to panic. Well, we knew there was trouble in Gaul—that was all we could say. Still, they'd follow you out of the town, and that would be unpleasant. But that didn't impress me nearly as much as the one old man.

We'd halted for half an hour and he came down from his fields, a countryman and a farmer. He had a speckled straw hat on, but it takes more than a dozen years' farming to get the look out of a man's back.

"The Twentieth," he said slowly, when he saw our badge of the boar, "the Valeria Victrix. Welcome, comrade!" so I knew at once that he'd served. I gave him the regulation salute and asked him a question, and his eyes glowed.

"Marcus Hostus," he said. "Centurion of the Third Cohort of the Second, twenty years ago." He pulled his tunic aside to show me the seamed scar.

"That was fighting the Welsh tribesmen," he said. "They were good fighters. After that, they gave me my land. But I still remember the taste of black beans in a helmet," and he laughed a high old man's laugh.

"Well," I said, "I wouldn't regret them. You've got a nice little place here." For he had.

He looked around at his fields. The woman had come to the door of the hut by then, with a half-grown girl beside her, and a couple of recruits were asking her for water.

"Yes," he said, "it's a nice little place and my sons are strong. There are two of them in the upper field. Are you halting for long, Centurion? I should like them to see the eagles before I die."

"Not for long," I said. "As a matter of fact, we're on our way to the seacoast. They seem to need us in Gaul."

"Oh," he said, "they need you in Gaul. But you'll be coming back."

"As Caesar wills it," I said. "You know what orders are, Centurion."

He looked at the eagles again.

"Yes," he said. "I know what orders are. The Valeria Victrix, the bulwark of the northwest. And you are marching to the ships—Oh, do not look at me, Centurion—I have been a centurion too. It must be a very great war that calls the Valeria Victrix from Britain."

"We have heard of such a war," I said, for he, too, had served with the eagles.

He nodded his old head once or twice. "Yes," he said, "a very great war. Even greater than the wars of Theodosius, for he did not take the Twentieth. Well, I can still use a sword."

I wanted to tell him that he would not have to use one, for there was the hut and the fields and the half-grown girl.

But, looking at him, the words stuck in my throat. He nodded again.

"When the eagles go, Britain falls," he said, very quietly. "If I were twenty years younger, I would go back to the Second—that would be good fighting. Or, perhaps, to the Sixth, at Eboracum—they will not withdraw the Sixth till the last of all. As it is, I die here, with my sons." He straightened himself. "Hail, Centurion of the Valeria Victrix and farewell," he said.

"Hail, Marcus Hostus, Centurion," I said, and they raised the eagles. I know that he watched us out of sight; though, again, I could not look back. It is true that he was an old man, and old men dream, but I was as glad that Agathocles had not heard his words.

For it seemed to me that Agathocles was always at my elbow and I grew very weary indeed of his company and his cough and what he called his philosophy. The march had done him no good—he was bonier than ever and his cheeks burned—but that did not stop his talkativeness. He was always pointing out to me little things I would hardly have noticed by myself— where a plowland had been left fallow or where a house or a barn still showed the scars of old burnings. By Hercules! As if a man couldn't plant wheat for a year without the empire's falling—but he'd point and nod his head. And then he'd keep talking—oh, about the states and the law they'd had in Greece, long before the city was founded. Well, I never argue with a man about the deeds of his ancestors—it only makes bad feeling. But I told him once, to shut him up, that I knew about Athens. A friend of mine had been stationed there once and said they had quite decent games for a provincial capital. His eyes flashed at that and he muttered something in his own tongue.

"Yes," he said. "They have decent games there. And buildings that make the sacred Forum at Rome—which I have seen, by the way, and which you have not seen—look like a child's playing with mud and rubble. That was when we had states and a law. Then we fought with each other, and it went—yes, even before the man from Macedon. And then you came and now, at last, it is your turn. Am I sorry or glad? I do not know. Sorry, I think, for the life is out of my people—they are clever and will always be clever, but the life is out of them. And I am not philosopher enough not to grieve when an end comes."

"Oh, talk as you like, Agathocles," I said, for I was resolved he shouldn't anger me again. "But you'd better not talk like that in front of the general."

"Thank you, Old Faithful," he said, and coughed till he nearly fell from his mule. "But I do not talk like that to the general—only to persons of rare intelligence, like yourself. The general does not like me very well, as it is, but I am still useful with the accounts. Perhaps, when we get to Gaul—if we go to Gaul—he will have me flayed or impaled. I believe those are Vandal customs. Yes, that is very probable, I think, if my cough does not kill me before. But, meanwhile, I must observe—we Greeks are so curious."

"Observe all you like," I said, "but the legion's shaking down very nicely, it seems to me."

"Yes, shaking down very nicely," he said. "Do you ever think of your deserter, who went back to Deva? No, I thought not. And yet he was the first effect of the cause I seek, and there have been others since." He chuckled quite cheerfully at that and went along reciting Greek poetry to himself till the cough took him again. The poetry was all about the fall of a city called Troy—he translated some of it to me, and it sounded quite well, if you care for that sort of thing, though, as I pointed out to him, our own Vergil had covered the same subjects, as I understand it.

We had turned toward the seacoast by then—we weren't going through Londinium after all. That disappointed our recruits, but of course the general was right about it. We'd kept excellent discipline so far, but it's a very different thing, letting the men loose in a capital. I was sorry not to see it again myself. I told the men that when they complained. This was southern country we passed through, very soft and gentle; though, on the coasts, there is danger. But, when we halted for the night, there had been no danger for years—it was a wide pocket of peace.

I remember the look of the big painted rooms of the villa, when I was summoned there. A very fine villa it was—it belonged to a rich man. They'd had Roman names so long, they'd forgotten their own stock, though the master looked British enough when you looked him full in the face. They had winged cupids painted on the walls of the dining room—they were sharpening arrows and driving little cars with doves—very pretty and bright. It must have been imported work—no Briton could paint like that. And the courtyard had orange trees in it, growing in tubs—I know what an orange tree costs, for my cousin was a gardener. A swarm of servants, too, better trained than our northern ones and sneakingly insolent, as rich men's servants are apt to be. But they were all honey to me, and sticky speeches—they knew better than to mock an officer on duty.

Well, I went into the room, and there was my general and the master of the house, both with wreaths around their heads in the old-fashioned way, and Agathocles making notes on his tablets in a corner and hiding his cough with his hand. My general had his wreath on crooked and he looked like a baited bear, though they must have had a good feed, and he liked wine. There were other people in the room—some sons and sons-in-law—all very well dressed, but a little shrill in their conversation, as that sort is apt to be, but the master of the house and my general were the ones I noticed.

My general called me in and told them who I was, while I stood at attention and Agathocles coughed. Then he said: "This is my senior centurion.... And how many leagues does the legion cover in a day, Centurion?"

I told him, though he knew well enough.

"Good," he said, in his thick Vandal accent. "And how many leagues would we cover in a day—let me see—accompanied by civilians, with litters and baggage?"

I told him; though, of course, he knew. It was less, of course; it made a decided difference. A legion does not march like the wind—that is not its business—but civilians slow everything up. Especially when there are women.

"As I thought," he said to the master of the villa. "As you see, it is quite impossible," and, in spite of his crooked wreath, his eyes were bleak and shrewd. Then arose a babble of talk and expostulation from the sons and the sons-in-law. I have heard such talk before—it is always the same. As I say, rich men are apt to think that all government, including the army, exists for their personal convenience. I stood at attention, waiting to be dismissed.

The master of the villa waited till the others had had their say. He was a strong man with a beaky nose, much stronger than his sons. He waited till the babble had ceased, his eyes calm, regarding our general. Then he said, in the smooth, careless voice of such men:

"The general forgets, perhaps, that I am a cousin of the legate. I merely ask protection for myself and my household. And we would be ready to move—well, within twenty-four hours. Yes, I can promise you, within twenty-four hours." There was such perfect assurance in his voice that I could have admired the man.

"I am sorry not to oblige a cousin of the legate," said my general, with his bear's eyes gleaming dully. "Unfortunately, I have my orders."

"And yet," said the master of the villa, charmingly, "a certain laxity—a certain interpretation, let us say…"

He left his words in the air—you could see he had done this sort of thing before, and always successfully. You could see that, all his life, he had been accustomed to rules being broken for him because of his place and name. I have liked other generals better than this general—after all, the Vandals are different from us—but I liked the way he shook his head now.

"I have my orders," he said, and lay hunched like a bear on his couch.

"Let us hope you will never regret your strict interpretation of them, General," the master of the villa said without rancor, and a cool wind blew through die room. I felt the cool wind on my own cheek, though I am a senior centurion and my appeal is to Caesar. The man was strong enough for that.

"Let us hope not," said my general gruffly, and rose. "Your hospitality has been very enjoyable." I must say, for a Vandal, he made his manners well. On the way out, the master of the villa stopped me unobtrusively.

"And what would it be worth, Centurion," he said in a low voice, "to carry a single man on your rolls who was not on your rolls before? A single man—I do not ask for more."

"It would be worth my head," I said; for though my general did not seem to be looking at me, I knew that he was looking.

The master of the villa nodded, and a curious, dazed look came over his strong face. "I thought so," he said, as if to himself. "And, after all, what then? My nephew in Gaul writes me that Gaul is not safe; my bankers in Rome write me that Rome itself is not safe. Will you tell me what place is safe if Rome is not safe any more?" he said in a stronger voice, and caught at my arm. I did not know how to answer him, so I kept silent. He looked, suddenly, very much older than he had when I entered the room.

"A king's ransom out at loan and the interest of the interest," he muttered. "And yet, how is a man to be safe? And my cousin is the legate, too—I have first-hand information. They will not bring back the legions—blood does not flow back, once it is spilt. And yet, how can I leave my house here, with everything so uncertain?"

It seemed a fine house to me, though not very defensible; but, even as he spoke, I could see the rain beating through the walls. I could see the walls fallen, and the naked people, the barbarians, huddled around a dim fire. I had not believed that possible before, but now I believed it. There was ruin in the face of that man. I could feel Agathocles tugging at my elbow and I went away—out through the courtyard where the orange trees stood in their tubs, and the bright fish played in the pool.

When we were back in our billets, Agathocles spoke to me.

"The general is pleased with you," he said. "He saw that they tried to bribe you, but you were not bribed. If you had been bribed, he would have had your head."

"Do I care for that?" I said, a little wildly. "What matters one head or another? But if Rome falls, something ends."

He nodded soberly, without coughing. "It is true," he said. "You had nothing but an arch, a road, an army and a law. And yet a man might walk from the east to the west because of it— yes, and speak the same tongue all the way. I do not admire you, but you were a great people."

"But tell me," I said, "why does it end?"

He shook his head. "I do not know," he said. "Men build and they go on building. And then the dream is shaken—it is shaken to bits by the storm. Afterwards, there follow darkness and the howling peoples. I think that will be for a long time. I meant to be a historian, when I first joined the eagles. I meant to write of the later wars of Rome as Thucydides wrote of the Greek wars.

But now my ink is dry and I have nothing to say."

"But," I said, "it is there—it is solid—it will last," for I thought of the country we had marched through, and the boy, unafraid, on his pony.

"Oh," said Agathocles, "it takes time for the night to fall—that is what people forget. Yes, even the master of your villa may die in peace. But there are still the two spirits in man—the spirit of building and the spirit of destruction. And when the second drives the faster horse, then the night comes on."

"You said you had a state and a law," I said. "Could you not have kept them?"

"Why, we could," said Agathocles, "but we did not. We had Pericles, but we shamed him. And now you and I—both Romans"—and he laughed and coughed— "we follow a hairy general to an unknown battle. And, beyond that, there is nothing."

"They say it is Alaric, the Goth," I said. "They say he marches on Rome," for, till then, except in jest, we had not spoken of these wars.

"Alaric, or another, what matters?" said Agathocles. "Who was that western chieftain—he called himself Niall of the Hundred Battles, did he not? And we put him down, in the end, but there were more behind him. Always more. It is time itself we fight, and no man wins against time. How long has the legion been in Britain, Centurion?"

"Three hundred and fifty years and eight," I said, for that is something that even children know.

"Yes," said Agathocles, "the Valeria Victrix. And who remembers the legions that were lost in Parthia and Germany? Who remembers their names?"

But by then I had come back to myself and did not wish to talk to him.

"All Greeks are eaters of wind," I said. "Caw like a crow, if you like; I do not listen."

"It does not matter to me," he said, with a shrug, and a cough. "I tell you, I shall be flayed before the ending, unless my cough ends it. No sensible general would let me live, after the notes I have taken tonight. But have it your own way."

I did not mean to let him see that he had shaken me, but he had. And when, six days later, we came to Anderida and the sea, I was shaken again. The ships should have been ready for us, but they were not, though our general raged like a bear, and we had to wait four days at Anderida. That was hard, for, in four days you get to know the look of a town. They had felt the strength of the sea pirates; they were not like Mid-Britain. I thought of my man at the villa and how he might die in peace, even as Agathocles had said. But all the time, the moss would be creeping on the stone and the rain beating at the door. Till, finally, the naked people gathered there, without knowledge—they would have forgotten the use of the furnace that kept the house warm in winter. and the baths that made men clean. And the fields of my veteran centurion of the Second, would go back to witch grass and crackleburs because they were too busy with killing to plant the wheat in the field. I even thought back to my deserter and saw him living, on one side or the other, but with memory of order and law and civilized things. Then that, too, would go, and his children would not remember it, except as a tale. I wanted to ask Agathocles what a race should leave to its kind, but I did not, for I knew he would talk of Greece, and I am a Roman.

Then we sailed, on a very clear day, with little wind, but enough to get us out of harbor. It came suddenly, as those things do, and we did not have time to think. I was very busy—it was only when we were ready to embark that I thought at all. I am a child of the camp and the legion is my hearth. But I knew, as we stood there, waiting, what we were leaving—the whole green, rainy, smoky, windy island, with its seas on either hand and its deep graves in the earth. We had been there three hundred and fifty and eight—we had been the Valeria Victrix. Now we followed a hairy general to an unknown battle, over the rim of the world, and we would win fights and lose them, but our time was over.

I heard the speech for the last time the British Latin. After that, it would only be the legion, wherever we went. Our general stood like a bear—he would take care of us as long as he could. Agathocles looked seasick already—his face was pinched and thin, and he coughed behind his hand. Before us lay the wide channel and the great darkness. And the Sixth still held Eboracum—I wished, for a moment, that I had been with the Sixth.

"Get your packs on board, you sons!" I shouted to the men.

As the crowd began to cheer, a little, I wanted to say to somebody, "Remember the Valeria Victrix! Remember our name!" But I could not have said it to anyone, and there was no time for those things.

The Blood of the Martyrs
(1936)

The man who expected to be shot lay with his eyes open, staring at the upper left-hand corner of his cell. He was fairly well over his last beating, and they might come for him any time now. There was a yellow stain in the cell corner near the ceiling; he had liked it at first, then disliked it; now he was coming back to liking it again.

He could see it more clearly with his glasses on, but he only put on his glasses for special occasions now—the first thing in the morning, and when they brought the food in, and for interviews with the General. The lenses of the glasses had been cracked in a beating some months before, and it strained his eyes to wear them too long. Fortunately, in his present life he had very few occasions demanding clear vision. But, nevertheless, the accident to his glasses worried him, as it worries all near-sighted people. You put your glasses on the first thing in the morning and the world leaps into proportion; if it does not do so, something is wrong with the world.

The man did not believe greatly in symbols, but his chief nightmare, nowadays, was an endless one in which, suddenly and without warning, a large piece of glass would drop out of one of the lenses and he would grope around the cell, trying to find it. He would grope very carefully and gingerly, for hours of darkness, but the end was always the same—the small, unmistakable crunch of irreplaceable glass beneath his heel or his knee. Then he would wake up sweating, with his hands cold. This dream alternated with the one of being shot, but he found no great benefit in the change.

As he lay there, you could see that he had an intellectual head—the head of a thinker or a scholar, old and bald, with the big, domed brow. It was, as a matter of fact, a well-known head; it had often appeared in the columns of newspapers and journals, sometimes when the surrounding text was in a language Professor Malzius could not read. The body, though stooped and worn, was still a strong peasant body and capable of surviving a good deal of ill-treatment, as his captors had found out. He had fewer teeth than when he came to prison, and both the ribs and the knee had been badly set, but these were minor matters. It also occurred to him that his blood count was probably poor. However, if he could ever get out and to a first-class hospital, he was probably good for at least ten years more of work. But, of course, he would not get out. They would shoot him before that, and it would be over.

Sometimes he wished passionately that it would be over—tonight—this moment; at other times he was shaken by the mere blind fear of death. The latter he tried to treat as he would have treated an attack of malaria, knowing that it was an attack, but not always with success. He should have been able to face it better than most—he was Gregor Malzius, the scientist—but that did not always help. The fear of death persisted, even when one had noted and classified it as a purely physical reaction. When he was out of here, he would be able to write a very instructive little paper on the fear of death. He could even do it here, if he had writing materials, but there was no use asking for those. Once they had been given him and he had spent two days quite happily. But they had torn up the work and spat upon it in front of his face. It was a childish thing to do, but it discouraged a man from working.

It seemed odd that he had never seen anybody shot, but he never had. During the war, his reputation and his bad eyesight had exempted him from active service. He had been bombed a couple of times when his reserve battalion was guarding the railway bridge, but that was quite different. You were not tied to a stake, and the airplanes were not trying to kill you as an individual. He knew the place where it was done here, of course. But prisoners did not see the executions, they merely heard, if the wind was from the right quarter.

He had tried again and again to visualize how it would be, but it always kept mixing with an old steel engraving he had seen in boyhood—the execution of William Walker, the American filibuster, in Honduras. William Walker was a small man with a white semi-Napoleonic face. He was standing, very correctly dressed, in front of an open grave, and before him a ragged line of picturesque natives were raising their muskets. When he was shot he would instantly and tidily fall into the grave, like a man dropping through a trap door; as a boy, the extreme neatness of the arrangement had greatly impressed Gregor Malzius. Behind the wall there were palm trees, and, somewhere off to the right, blue and warm, the Caribbean Sea. It would not be like that at all, for his own execution; and yet, whenever he thought of it, he thought of it as being like that.

Well, it was his own fault. He could have accepted the new regime; some respectable people had done that. He could have fled the country; many honorable people had. A scientist should be concerned with the eternal, not with transient political phenomena; and a scientist should be able to live anywhere. But thirty years at the university were thirty years, and, after all, he was Malzius, one of the first biochemists in the world. To the last, he had not believed that they would touch him. Well, he had been wrong about that.

The truth, of course, was the truth. One taught it or one did not teach it. If one did not teach it, it hardly mattered what one did. But he had no quarrel with any established government; he was willing to run up a flag every Tuesday, as long as they let him alone. Most people were fools, and one government was as good as another for them—it had taken them twenty years to accept his theory of cell mutation. Now, if he'd been like his friend Bonnard—a fellow who signed protests, attended meetings for the cause of world peace, and generally played the fool in public—they'd have had some reason to complain. An excellent man in his field, Bonnard—none better—but, outside of it, how deplorably like an actor, with his short gray beard, his pink cheeks and his impulsive enthusiasms! Any government could put a fellow like Bonnard in prison—though it would be an injury to science and, therefore, wrong. For that matter, he thought grimly, Bonnard would enjoy being a martyr. He'd walk gracefully to the execution post with a begged cigarette in his mouth, and some theatrical last quip. But Bonnard was safe in his own land—doubtless writing heated and generous articles on The Case of Professor Malzius—and he, Malzius, was the man who was going to be shot. He would like a cigarette, too, on his way to execution; he had not smoked in five months. But he certainly didn't intend to ask for one, and they wouldn't think of offering him any. That was the difference between him and Bonnard.

His mind went back with longing to the stuffy laboratory and stuffier lecture hall at the university; his feet yearned for the worn steps he had climbed ten thousand times, and his eyes for the long steady look through the truthful lens into worlds too tiny for the unaided eye. They had called him "The Bear" and "Old Prickly," but they had fought to work under him, the best of the young men. They said he would explain the Last Judgment in terms of cellular phenomena, but they had crowded to his lectures. It was Williams, the Englishman, who had made up the legend that he carried a chocolate éclair and a set of improper post cards in his battered brief case. Quite untrue, of course—chocolate always made him ill, and he had never looked at an improper post card in his life. And Williams would never know that he knew the legend, too; for Williams had been killed long ago in the war. For a moment, Professor Malzius felt blind hate at the thought of an excellent scientific machine like Williams being smashed in a war. But blind hate was an improper emotion for a scientist, and he put it aside.

He smiled grimly again; they hadn't been able to break up his classes—lucky he was The Bear! He'd seen one colleague hooted from his desk by a band of determined young hoodlums—too bad, but if a man couldn't keep order in his own classroom, he'd better get out. They'd wrecked his own laboratory, but not while he was there.

It was so senseless, so silly. "In God's name," he said reasonably, to no one, "what sort of conspirator do you think I would make? A man of my age and habits! I am interested in cellular phenomena!" And yet they were beating him because he would not tell about the boys. As if he had even paid attention to half the nonsense! There were certain passwords and greetings—a bar of music you whistled, entering a restaurant; the address of a firm that specialized, ostensibly, in vacuum cleaners. But they were not his own property. They belonged to the young men who had trusted The Bear. He did not know what half of them meant, and the one time he had gone to a meeting, he had felt like a fool. For they were fools and childish—playing the childish games of conspiracy that people like Bonnard enjoyed. Could they even make a better world than the present? He doubted it extremely. And yet, he could not betray them; they had come to him, looking over their shoulders, with darkness in their eyes.

A horrible, an appalling thing—to be trusted. He had no wish to be a guide and counselor of young men. He wanted to do his work. Suppose they were poor and ragged and oppressed; he had been a peasant himself, he had eaten black bread. It was by his own efforts that he was Professor Malzius. He did not wish the confidences of boys like Gregopolous and the others—for, after all, what was Gregopolous? An excellent and untiring laboratory assistant—and a laboratory assistant he would remain to the end of his days. He had pattered about the laboratory like a fox terrier, with a fox terrier's quick bright eyes. Like a devoted dog, he had made a god of Professor Malzius. "I don't want your problems, man. I don't want to know what you are doing outside the laboratory." But Gregopolous had brought his problems and his terrible trust none the less, humbly and proudly, like a fox terrier with a bone. After that—well, what was a man to do?

He hoped they would get it over with, and quickly. The world should be like a chemical formula, full of reason and logic. Instead, there were all these young men, and their eyes. They conspired, hopelessly and childishly, for what they called freedom against the new regime. They wore no overcoats in winter and were often hunted and killed. Even if they did not conspire, they had miserable little love affairs and ate the wrong food—yes, even before, at the university, they had been the same. Why the devil would they not accept? Then they could do their work. Of course, a great many of them would not be allowed to accept—they had the wrong ideas or the wrong politics—but then they could run away. If Malzius, at twenty, had had to run from his country, he would still have been a scientist. To talk of a free world was a delusion; men were not free in the world. Those who wished got a space of time to get their work done. That was all. And yet, he had not accepted—he did not know why.

Now he heard the sound of steps along the corridor. His body began to quiver and the places where he had been beaten hurt him. He noted it as an interesting reflex. Sometimes they merely flashed the light in the cell and passed by. On the other hand, it might be death. It was a hard question to decide.

The lock creaked, the door opened. "Get up, Malzius!" said the hard, bright voice of the guard. Gregor Malzius got up, a little stiffly, but quickly.

"Put on your glasses, you old fool!" said the guard, with a laugh. "You are going to the General."

Professor Malzius found the stone floors of the corridor uneven, though he knew them well enough. Once or twice the guard struck him, lightly and without malice, as one strikes an old horse with a whip. The blows were familiar and did not register on Professor Malzius' consciousness; he merely felt proud of not stumbling. He was apt to stumble; once he had hurt his knee.

He noticed, it seemed to him, an unusual tenseness and officiousness about his guard. Once, even, in a brightly lighted corridor the guard moved to strike him, but refrained. However, that, too, happened occasionally, with one guard or another, and Professor Malzius merely noted the fact. It was a small fact, but an important one in the economy in which he lived.

But there could be no doubt that something unusual was going on in the castle. There were more guards than usual, many of them strangers. He tried to think, carefully, as he walked, if it could be one of the new national holidays. It was hard to keep track of them all. The General might be in a good humor. Then they would merely have a cat-and-mouse conversation for half an hour and nothing really bad would happen. Once, even, there had been a cigar. Professor Malzius, the scientist, licked his lips at the thought.

Now he was being turned over to a squad of other guards, with salutings. This was really unusual; Professor Malzius bit his mouth, inconspicuously. He had the poignant distrust of a monk or an old prisoner at any break in routine. Old prisoners are your true conservatives; they only demand that the order around them remains exactly the same.

It alarmed him as well that the new guards did not laugh at him. New guards almost always laughed when they saw him for the first time. He was used to the laughter and missed it—his throat felt dry. He would have liked, just once, to eat at the university restaurant before he died. It was bad food, ill cooked and starchy, food good enough for poor students and professors, but he would have liked to be there, in the big smoky room that smelt of copper boilers and cabbage, with a small cup of bitter coffee before him and a cheap cigarette. He did not ask for his dog or his notebooks, the old photographs in his bedroom, his incomplete experiments or his freedom. Just to lunch once more at the university restaurant and have people point out The Bear. It seemed a small thing to ask, but of course it was quite impossible.

"Halt!" said a voice, and he halted. There were, for the third time, salutings. Then the door of the General's office opened and he was told to go in.

He stood, just inside the door, in the posture of attention, as he had been taught. The crack in the left lens of his glasses made a crack across the room, and his eyes were paining him already, but he paid no attention to that. There was the familiar figure of the General, with his air of a well-fed and extremely healthy tomcat, and there was another man, seated at the General's desk. He could not see the other man very well—the crack made him bulge and waver—but he did not like his being there.

"Well, professor," said the General, in an easy, purring voice.

Malzius's entire body jerked. He had made a fearful, an unpardonable omission. He must remedy it at once. "Long live the state," he shouted in a loud thick voice, and saluted. He knew, bitterly, that his salute was ridiculous and that he looked ridiculous, making it. But perhaps the General would laugh—he had done so before. Then everything would be all right, for it was not quite as easy to beat a man after you had laughed at him.

The General did not laugh. He made a half turn instead, toward the man at the desk. The gesture said, "You see, he is well trained." It was the gesture of a man of the world, accustomed to deal with unruly peasants and animals—the gesture of a man fitted to be General.

The man at the desk paid no attention to the General's gesture. He lifted his head, and Malzius saw him more clearly and with complete unbelief. It was not a man but a picture come alive. Professor Malzius had seen the picture a hundred times; they had made him salute and take off his hat in front of it, when he had had a hat. Indeed, the picture had presided over his beatings. The man himself was a little smaller, but the picture was a good picture. There were many dictators in the world, and this was one type. The face was white, beaky and semi-Napoleonic; the lean, military body sat squarely in its chair. The eyes dominated the face, and the mouth was rigid.

"I remember also a hypnotist, and a woman Charcot showed me, at his clinic in Paris," thought Professor Malzius. "But there is also, obviously, an endocrine unbalance." Then his thoughts stopped.

"Tell the man to come closer," said the man at the desk. "Can he hear me? Is he deaf?"

"No, Your Excellency," said the General, with enormous, purring respect. "But he is a little old, though perfectly healthy.... Are you not, Professor Malzius?"

"Yes, I am perfectly healthy. I am very well treated here," said Professor Malzius, in his loud thick voice. They were not going to catch him with traps like that, not even by dressing up somebody as the Dictator. He fixed his eyes on the big old-fashioned inkwell on the General's desk—that, at least, was perfectly sane.

"Come closer," said the man at the desk to Professor Malzius, and the latter advanced till he could almost touch the inkwell with his fingers. Then he stopped with a jerk, hoping he had done right. The movement removed the man at the desk from the crack in his lenses, and Professor Malzius knew suddenly that it was true. This was, indeed, the Dictator, this man with the rigid mouth. He began to talk.

"I have been very well treated here and the General has acted with the greatest consideration," he said. "But I am Professor Gregor Malzius—professor of biochemistry. For thirty years I have lectured at the university; I am a fellow of the Royal Society, a corresponding member of the Academy of Sciences at Berlin, at Rome, at Boston, at Paris and Stockholm. I have received the Nottingham Medal, the Lamarck Medal, the Order of St. John of Portugal and the Nobel Prize. I think my blood count is low, but I have received a great many degrees and my experiments on the migratory cells are not finished. I do not wish to complain of my treatment, but I must continue my experiments."

He stopped, like a clock that has run down, surprised to hear the sound of his own voice. He noted, in one part of his mind, that the General had made a move to silence him, but had himself been silenced by the Dictator.

"Yes, Professor Malzius," said the man at the desk, in a harsh, toneless voice. "There has been a regrettable error." The rigid face stared at Professor Malzius. Professor Malzius stared back. He did not say anything.

"In these days," said the Dictator, his voice rising, "the nation demands the submission of every citizen. Encircled by jealous foes, our reborn land yet steps forward toward her magnificent destiny." The words continued for some time, the voice rose and fell. Professor Malzius listened respectfully; he had heard the words many times before and they had ceased to have meaning to him. He was thinking of certain cells of the body that rebel against the intricate processes of Nature and set up their own bellicose state. Doubtless they, too, have a destiny, he thought, but in medicine it is called cancer.

"Jealous and spiteful tongues in other countries have declared that it is our purpose to wipe out learning and science," concluded the Dictator. "That is not our purpose. After the cleansing, the rebirth. We mean to move forward to the greatest science in the world—our own science, based on the enduring principles of our nationhood." He ceased abruptly, his eyes fell into their dream. Very like the girl Charcot showed me in my young days, thought Professor Malzius; there was first the ebullition, then the calm.

"I was part of the cleansing? You did not mean to hurt me?" he asked timidly.

"Yes, Professor Malzius," said the General, smiling, "you were part of the cleansing. Now that is over. His Excellency has spoken."

"I do not understand," said Professor Malzius, gazing at the fixed face of the man behind the desk.

"It is very simple," said the General. He spoke in a slow careful voice, as one speaks to a deaf man or a child. "You are a distinguished man of science—you have received the Nobel Prize. That was a service to the state. You became, however, infected by the wrong political ideas. That was treachery to the state. You had, therefore, as decreed by His Excellency, to pass through a certain period for probation and rehabilitation. But that, we believe, is finished."

"You do not wish to know the names of the young men any more?" said Professor Malzius. "You do not want the addresses?"

"That is no longer of importance," said the General patiently. "There is no longer opposition. The leaders were caught and executed three weeks ago."

"There is no longer opposition," repeated Professor Malzius.

"At the trial, you were not even involved."

"I was not even involved," said Professor Malzius. "Yes."

"Now," said the General, with a look at the Dictator, "we come to the future. I will be frank—the new state is frank with its citizens."

"It is so," said the Dictator, his eyes still sunk in his dream.

"There has been—let us say—a certain agitation in foreign countries regarding Professor Malzius," said the General, his eyes still fixed on the Dictator. "That means nothing, of course. Nevertheless, your acquaintance, Professor Bonnard, and others have meddled in matters that do not concern them."

"They asked after me?" said Professor Malzius, with surprise. "It is true, my experiments were reaching a point that—"

"No foreign influence could turn us from our firm purpose," said the Dictator. "But it is our firm purpose to show our nation first in science and culture as we have already shown her first in manliness and statehood. For that reason, you are here, Professor Malzius." He smiled.

Professor Malzius stared. His cheeks began to tremble.

"I do not understand," said Professor Malzius. "You will give me my laboratory back?"

"Yes," said the Dictator, and the General nodded as one nods to a stupid child.

Professor Malzius passed a hand across his brow.

"My post at the university?" he said. "My experiments?"

"It is the purpose of our regime to offer the fullest encouragement to our loyal sons of science," said the Dictator.

"First of all," said Professor Malzius, "I must go to a hospital. My blood count is poor. But that will not take long." His voice had become impatient and his eyes glowed. "Then—my notebooks were burned, I suppose. That was silly, but we can start in again. I have a very good memory, an excellent memory. The theories are in my head, you know," and he tapped it. "I must have assistants, of course; little Gregopolous was my best one—"

"The man Gregopolous has been executed," said the General, in a stern voice. "You had best forget him."

"Oh," said Professor Malzius. "Well, then, I must have someone else. You see, these are important experiments. There must be some young men—clever ones—they cannot all be dead. I will know them." He laughed a little, nervously. "The Bear always got the pick of the crop," he said. "They used to call me The Bear, you know." He stopped and looked at them for a moment with ghastly eyes. "You are not fooling me?" he said. He burst into tears.

When he recovered he was alone in the room with the General. The General was looking at him as he himself had looked once at strange forms of life under the microscope, with neither disgust nor attraction, but with great interest.

"His Excellency forgives your unworthy suggestion," he said. "He knows you are overwrought."

"Yes," said Professor Malzius. He sobbed once and dried his glasses.

"Come, come," said the General, with a certain bluff heartiness. "We mustn't have our new president of the National Academy crying. It would look badly in the photographs."

"President of the Academy?" said Professor Malzius quickly. "Oh, no; I mustn't be that. They make speeches; they have administrative work. But I am a scientist, a teacher."

"I'm afraid you can't very well avoid it," said the General, still heartily, though he looked at Professor Malzius. "Your induction will be quite a ceremony. His Excellency himself will preside. And you will speak on the new glories of our science. It will be a magnificent answer to the petty and jealous criticisms of our neighbors. Oh, you needn't worry about the speech," he added quickly. "It will be prepared; you will only have to read it. His Excellency thinks of everything."

"Very well," said Professor Malzius; "and then may I go back to my work?"

"Oh, don't worry about that," said the General, smiling. "I'm only a simple soldier; I don't know about those things. But you'll have plenty of work."

"The more the better," said Malzius eagerly. "I still have ten good years."

He opened his mouth to smile, and a shade of dismay crossed the General's face.

"Yes," he said, as if to himself. "The teeth must be attended to. At once. And a rest, undoubtedly, before the photographs are taken. Milk. You are feeling sufficiently well, Professor Malzius?"

"I am very happy," said Professor Malzius. "I have been very well treated and I come of peasant stock."

"Good," said the General. He paused for a moment, and spoke in a more official voice.

"Of course, it is understood, Professor Malzius—" he said.

"Yes?" said Professor Malzius. "I beg your pardon. I was thinking of something else."

"It is understood, Professor Malzius," repeated the General, "that your—er—rehabilitation in the service of the state is a permanent matter. Naturally, you will be under observation, but, even so, there must be no mistake."

"I am a scientist," said Professor Malzius impatiently. "What have I to do with politics? If you wish me to take oaths of loyalty, I will take as many as you wish."

"I am glad you take that attitude," said the General, though he looked at Professor Malzius curiously. "I may say that I regret the unpleasant side of our interviews. I trust you bear no ill will."

"Why should I be angry?" said Professor Malzius. "You were told to do one thing. Now you are told to do another. That is all."

"It is not quite so simple as that," said the General rather stiffly. He looked at Professor Malzius for a third time. "And I'd have sworn you were one of the stiff-necked ones," he said. "Well, well, every man has his breaking point, I suppose. In a few moments you will receive the final commands of His Excellency. Tonight you will go to the capitol and speak over the radio. You will have no difficulty there—the speech is written. But it will put a quietus on the activities of our friend Bonnard and the question that has been raised in the British Parliament. Then a few weeks of rest by the sea and the dental work, and then, my dear president of the National Academy, you will be ready to undertake your new duties. I congratulate you and hope we shall meet often under pleasant auspices." He bowed from the waist to Malzius, the bow of a man of the world, though there was still something feline in his mustaches. Then he stood to attention, and Malzius, too, for the Dictator had come into the room.

"It is settled?" said the Dictator. "Good. Gregor Malzius, I welcome you to the service of the new state. You have cast your errors aside and are part of our destiny."

"Yes," said Professor Malzius, "I will be able to do my work now."

The Dictator frowned a little.

"You will not only be able to continue your invaluable researches," he said, "but you will also be able—and it will be part of your duty—to further our national ideals. Our reborn nation must rule the world for the world's good. There is a fire within us that is not in other stocks. Our civilization must be extended everywhere. The future wills it. It will furnish the subject of your first discourse as president of the Academy."

"But," said Professor Malzius, in a low voice, "I am not a soldier. I am a biochemist. I have no experience in these matters you speak of."

The Dictator nodded. "You are a distinguished man of science," he said. "You will prove that our women must bear soldiers, our men abandon this nonsense of republics and democracies for trust in those born to rule them. You will prove by scientific law that certain races—our race in particular—are destined to rule the world. You will prove they are destined to rule by the virtues of war, and that war is part of our heritage."

"But," said Professor Malzius, "it is not like that. I mean," he said, "one looks and watches in the laboratory. One waits for a long time. It is a long process, very long. And then, if the theory is not proved, one discards the theory. That is the way it is done. I probably do not explain it well. But I am a biochemist; I do not know how to look for the virtues of one race against another, and I can prove nothing about war, except that it kills. If I said anything else, the whole world would laugh at me."

"Not one in this nation would laugh at you," said the Dictator.

"But if they do not laugh at me when I am wrong, there is no science," said Professor Malzius, knotting his brows. He paused.

"Do not misunderstand me," he said earnestly. "I have ten years of good work left; I want to get back to my laboratory. But, you see, there are the young men—if I am to teach the young men."

He paused again, seeing their faces before him. There were many. There was Williams, the Englishman, who had died in the war, and little Gregopolous with the fox-terrier eyes. There were all who had passed through his classrooms, from the stupidest to the best. They had shot little Gregopolous for treason, but that did not alter the case. From all over the world they had come—he remembered the Indian student and the Chinese. They wore cheap overcoats, they were hungry for knowledge, they ate the bad, starchy food of the poor restaurants, they had miserable little love affairs and played childish games of politics, instead of doing their work. Nevertheless, a few were promising—all must be given the truth. It did not matter if they died, but they must be given the truth. Otherwise there could be no continuity and no science.

He looked at the Dictator before him—yes, it was a hysteric face. He would know how to deal with it in his classroom—but such faces should not rule countries or young men. One was willing to go through a great many meaningless ceremonies in order to do one's work—wear a uniform or salute or be president of the Academy. That did not matter; it was part of the due to Caesar. But not to tell lies to young men on one's own subject. After all, they had called him The Bear and said he carried improper post cards in his brief case. They had given him their terrible confidence—not for love or kindness, but because they had found him honest. It was too late to change.

The Dictator looked sharply at the General. "I thought this had been explained to Professor Malzius," he said.

"Why, yes," said Professor Malzius. "I will sign any papers.

I assure you I am not interested in politics—a man like myself, imagine! One state is as good as another. And I miss my tobacco—I have not smoked in five months. But, you see, one cannot be a scientist and tell lies."

He looked at the two men.

"What happens if I do not?" he said, in a low voice. But, looking at the Dictator, he had his answer. It was a fanatic face.

"Why, we shall resume our conversations, Professor Malzius," said the General, with a simper.

"Then I shall be beaten again," said Professor Malzius. He stated what he knew to be a fact.

"The process of rehabilitation is obviously not quite complete," said the General, "but perhaps, in time—"

"It will not be necessary," said Professor Malzius. "I cannot be beaten again." He stared wearily around the room. His shoulders straightened—it was so he had looked in the classroom when they had called him The Bear. "Call your other officers in," he said in a clear voice. "There are papers for me to sign. I should like them all to witness."

"Why—" said the General. "Why—" He looked doubtfully at the Dictator.

An expression of gratification appeared on the lean, semi-Napoleonic face. A white hand, curiously limp, touched the hand of Professor Malzius.

"You will feel so much better, Gregor," said the hoarse, tense voice. "I am so very glad you have given in."

"Why, of course, I give in," said Gregor Malzius. "Are you not the Dictator? And besides, if I do not, I shall be beaten again. And I cannot—you understand?—I cannot be beaten again."

He paused, breathing a little. But already the room was full of other faces. He knew them well, the hard faces of the new regime. But youthful some of them too.

The Dictator was saying something with regard to receiving the distinguished scientist, Professor Gregor Malzius, into the service of the state.

"Take the pen," said the General in an undertone. "The inkwell is there, Professor Malzius. Now you may sign."

Professor Malzius stood, his fingers gripping the big, old-fashioned inkwell. It was full of ink—the servants of the Dictator were very efficient. They could shoot small people with the eyes of fox terriers for treason, but their trains arrived on time and their inkwells did not run dry.

"The state," he said, breathing. "Yes. But science does not know about states. And you are a little man—a little, unimportant man."

Then, before the General could stop him, he had picked up the inkwell and thrown it in the Dictator's face. The next moment the General's fist caught him on the side of the head and he fell behind the desk to the floor. But lying there, through his cracked glasses, he could still see the grotesque splashes of ink on the Dictator's face and uniform, and the small cut above his eye where the blood was gathering. They had not fired; he had thought he would be too close to the Dictator for them to fire in time.

"Take that man out and shoot him. At once," said the Dictator in a dry voice. He did not move to wipe the stains from his uniform—and for that Professor Malzius admired him. They rushed then, each anxious to be first. But Professor Malzius made no resistance.

As he was being hustled along the corridors, he fell now and then. On the second fall, his glasses were broken completely, but that did not matter to him. They were in a great hurry, he thought, but all the better—one did not have to think while one could not see.

Now and then he heard his voice make sounds of discomfort, but his voice was detached from himself. There was little Gregopolous—he could see him very plainly—and Williams, with his fresh English coloring—and all the men whom he had taught.

He had given them nothing but work and the truth; they had given him their terrible trust. If he had been beaten again, he might have betrayed them. But he had avoided that.

He felt a last weakness—a wish that someone might know. They would not, of course; he would have died of typhoid in the castle and there would be regretful notices in the newspapers. And then he would be forgotten, except for his work, and that was as it should be. He had never thought much of martyrs—hysterical people in the main. Though he'd like Bonnard to have known about the ink; it was in the coarse vein of humor that Bonnard could not appreciate. But then, he was a peasant; Bonnard had often told him so.

They were coming out into an open courtyard now; he felt the fresh air of outdoors. "Gently," he said. "A little gently. What's the haste?" But already they were tying him to the post. Someone struck him in the face and his eyes watered. "A schoolboy covered with ink," he muttered through his lost teeth. "A hysterical schoolboy too. But you cannot kill truth."

They were not good last words, and he knew that they were not. He must try to think of better ones—not shame Bonnard. But now they had a gag in his mouth; just as well; it saved him the trouble.

His body ached, bound against the post, but his sight and his mind were clearer. He could make out the evening sky, gray with fog, the sky that belonged to no country, but to all the world.

He could make out the gray high buttress of the castle. They had made it a jail, but it would not always be a jail. Perhaps in time it would not even exist. But if a little bit of truth were gathered, that would always exist, while there were men to remember and rediscover it. It was only the liars and the cruel who always failed.

Sixty years ago, he had been a little boy, eating black bread and thin cabbage soup in a poor house. It had been a bitter life, but he could not complain of it. He had had some good teachers and they had called him The Bear.

The gag hurt his mouth—they were getting ready now. There had been a girl called Anna once; he had almost forgotten her. And his rooms had smelt a certain way and he had had a dog. It did not matter what they did with the medals. He raised his head and looked once more at the gray foggy sky. In a moment there would be no thought, but, while there was thought, one must remember and note. His pulse rate was lower than he would have expected and his breathing oddly even, but those were not the important things. The important thing was beyond, in the gray sky that had no country, in the stones of the earth and the feeble human spirit. The important thing was truth.

"Ready!" called the officer. "Aim! Fire!" But Professor Malzius did not hear the three commands of the officer. He was thinking about the young men.

Into Egypt
(1939)

It had finally been decided to let them go and now, for three days, they had been passing. The dust on the road to the frontier had not settled for three days or nights. But the strictest orders had been given and there were very few incidents. There could easily have been more.

Even the concentration camps had been swept clean, for this thing was to be final. After it, the State could say "How fearless we are—we let even known conspirators depart." It is true that, in the case of those in the concentration camps, there had been a preliminary rectification—a weeding, so to speak. But the news of that would not be officially published for some time and the numbers could always be disputed. If you kill a few people, they remain persons with names and identities, but, if you kill in the hundreds, there is simply a number for most of those who read the newspapers. And, once you start arguing about numbers, you begin to wonder if the thing ever happened at all. This too had been foreseen.

In fact, everything had been foreseen—and with great acuteness. There had been the usual diplomatic tension, solved, finally, by the usual firm stand. At the last moment, the other Powers had decided to co-operate. They had done so unwillingly, grudgingly, and with many representations, but they had done so. It was another great victory. And everywhere the trains rolled and the dust rose on the roads, for, at last and at length, the Accursed People were going. Every one of them, man, woman and child, to the third and the fourth generation—every one of them with a drop of that blood in his veins. And this was the end of it all and, by sunset on the third day, the land would know them no more. It was another great victory—perhaps the greatest. There would be a week of celebration after it, with appropriate ceremonies and speeches, and the date would be marked in the new calendar, with the date of the founding of the State and other dates.

Nevertheless, and even with the noteworthy efficiency of which the State was so proud, any mass evacuation is bound to be a complicated and fatiguing affair. The lieutenant stationed at the crossroads found it so—he was young and in the best of health but the strain was beginning to tell on him, though he would never have admitted it. He had been a little nervous at first—a little nervous and exceedingly anxious that everything should go according to plan. After all, it was an important post, the last crossroads before the frontier. A minor road, of course—they'd be busier on the main highways and at the ports of embarkation—but a last crossroads, nevertheless. He couldn't flatter himself it was worth a decoration—the bigwigs would get those. But, all the same, he was expected to evacuate so many thousands—he knew the figures by heart. Easy enough to say one had only to follow the plan! That might do for civilians—an officer was an officer. Would he show himself enough of an officer, would he make a fool of himself in front of his men? Would he even, perhaps, by some horrible, unforeseen mischance, get his road clogged with fleeing humanity till they had to send somebody over from Staff to straighten the tangle out? The thought was appalling.

He could see it happening in his mind—as a boy, he had been imaginative. He could hear the staff officer's words while he stood at attention, eyes front. One's first real command and a black mark on one's record! Yes, even if it was only police work—that didn't matter—a citizen of the State, a member of the Party must be held to an unflinching standard. If one failed to meet that standard there was nothing left in life. His throat had been dry and his movements a little jerky as he made his last dispositions and saw the first black specks begin to struggle toward the crossroads.

He could afford to laugh at that now, if he had had time. He could even afford to remember old Franz, his orderly, trying to put the brandy in his coffee, that first morning. "It's a chilly morning, Lieutenant," but there had been a question in Franz's eyes. He'd refused the brandy, of course, and told Franz off properly, too. The new State did not depend on Dutch courage but on the racial valor of its citizens. And the telling-off had helped—it had made his own voice firmer and given a little fillip of anger to his pulse. But Franz was an old soldier and imperturbable. What was it he had said, later? "The lieutenant must not worry. Civilians are always sheep—it is merely a matter of herding them." An improper remark, of course, to one's lieutenant, but it had helped settle his mind and make it cooler. Yes, an orderly like Franz was worth something, once one learned the knack of keeping him in his place.

Then they had begun to come, slowly, stragglingly, not like soldiers. He couldn't remember who had been the first. It was strange but he could not—he had been sure that he would remember. Perhaps a plodding family, with the scared children looking at him—perhaps one of the old men with long beards and burning eyes. But, after three days, they all mixed, the individual faces. As Franz had said, they became civilian sheep—sheep that one must herd and keep moving, keep moving always through day and night, moving on to the frontier. As they went, they wailed. When the wailing grew too loud, one took measures; but, sooner or later it always began again. It would break out down the road, die down as it came toward the post. It seemed to come out of their mouths without their knowledge—the sound of broken wood, of wheat ground between stones. He had tried to stop it completely at first, now he no longer bothered. And yet there were many—a great many—who did not wail.

At first, it had been interesting to see how many different types there were. He had not thought to find such variety among the Accursed People—one had one's own mental picture, reinforced by the pictures in the newspapers. But, seeing them was different. They were not at all like the picture. They were tall and short, plump and lean, black-haired, yellow-haired, red-haired. It was obvious, even under the film of dust, that some had been rich, others poor, some thoughtful, others active. Indeed, it was often hard to tell them, by the looks. But that was not his affair—his affair was to keep them moving. All the same, it gave you a shock, sometimes, at first.

Perhaps the queerest thing was that they all looked so ordinary, so much a part of everyday. That was because one had been used to seeing them—it could be no more than that. But, under the film of dust and heat, one would look at a face. And then one would think, unconsciously, "Why, what is that fellow doing, so far from where he lives? Why, for heaven's sake, is he straggling along this road? He doesn't look happy." Then the mind would resume control and one would remember. But the thought would come, now and then, without orders from the mind.

He had seen very few that he knew. That was natural—he came from the South. He had seen Willi Schneider, to be sure—that had been the second day and it was very dusty. When he was a little boy, very young, he had played in Willi's garden with Willi, in the summers, and, as they had played, there had come to them, through the open window, the ripple of a piano and the clear, rippling flow of Willi's mother's voice. It was not a great voice—not a Brunhild voice—but beautiful in *lieder* and beautifully sure. She had sung at their own house; that was odd to remember. Of course, her husband had not been one of them—a councilor, in fact. Needless to say, that had been long before the discovery that even the faintest trace of that blood tainted. As for Willi and himself, they had been friends—yes, even through the first year or so at school. Both of them had meant to run away and be cowboys, and they had had a secret password. Naturally, things had changed, later on.

For a horrible moment, he had thought that Willi would speak to him—recall the warm air of summer and the smell of linden and those young, unmanly days. But Willi did not. Their eyes met, for an instant, then both had looked away. Willi was helping an old woman along, an old woman who muttered fretfully as she walked, like a cat with sore paws. They were both of them covered with dust and the old woman went slowly. Willi's mother had walked with a quick step and her voice had not been cracked or fretful. After play, she had given them both cream buns, laughing and moving her hands, in a bright green dress. It was not permitted to think further of Willi Schneider.

That was the only real acquaintance but there were other, recognizable faces. There was the woman who had kept the newsstand, the brisk little waiter at the summer hotel, the taxi chauffeur with the squint and the heart specialist. Then there was the former scientist—one could still tell him from his pictures—and the actor one had often seen. That was all that one knew and not all on the same day. That was enough. He had not imagined the taxi chauffeur with a wife and children and that the youngest child should be lame. That had surprised him—surprised him almost as much as seeing the heart specialist walking along the road like any man. It had surprised him, also, to see the scientist led along between two others and to recognize the fact that he was mad.

But that also mixed with the dust—the endless, stifling cloud of the dust, the endless, moving current. The dust got in one's throat and one's eyes—it was hard to cut, even with brandy, from one's throat. It lay on the endless bundles people carried; queer bundles, bulging out at the ends, with here a ticking clock, and there a green bunch of carrots. It lay on the handcarts a few of them pushed—the handcarts bearing the sort of goods that one would snatch, haphazard, from a burning house. It rose and whirled and penetrated—it was never still. At night, slashed by the efficient searchlights that made the night bright as day, it was still a mist above the road. As for sleep—well, one slept when one could, for a couple of hours after midnight, when they too slept, ungracefully, in heaps and clumps by the road. But, except for the first night, he could not even remember Franz pulling his boots off.

His men had been excellent, admirable, indefatigable. That was, of course, due to the Leader and the State, but still, he would put it in his report. They had kept the stream moving, always. The attitude had been the newly prescribed one—not that of punishment, richly as that was deserved, but of complete aloofness, as if the Accursed People did not even exist. Naturally, now and then, the men had had their fun. One could not blame them for that—some of the incidents had been extremely comic. There had been the old woman with the hen—a comedy character. Of course, she had not been permitted to keep the hen. They should have taken it away from her at the inspection point. But she had looked very funny, holding on to the squawking chicken by the tail feathers, with the tears running down her face.

Yes, the attitude of the men would certainly go in his report. He would devote a special paragraph to the musicians also—they had been indefatigable. They had played the prescribed tunes continually, in spite of the dust and the heat. One would hope that those tunes would sink into the hearts of the Accursed People, to be forever a warning and a memory. Particularly if they happened to know the words. But one could never be sure about people like that.

Staff cars had come four times, the first morning, and once there had been a general. He had felt nervous, when they came, but there had been no complaint. After that, they had let him alone, except for an occasional visit—that must mean they thought him up to his work. Once, even, the road had been almost clear, for a few minutes—he was moving them along faster than they did at the inspection point. The thought had gone to his head for an instant, but he kept cool—and, soon enough, the road had been crowded again.

As regarded casualties—he could not keep the exact figure in his head, but it was a minor one. A couple of heart attacks—one of the man who had been a judge, or so the others said. Unpleasant but valuable to see the life drain out of a face like that. He had made himself watch it—one must harden oneself. They had wanted to remove the body—of course, that had not been allowed. The women taken in childbirth had been adequately dealt with—one could do nothing to assist. But he had insisted, for decency's sake, on a screen, and Franz had been very clever at rigging one up. Only two of those had died, the rest had gone on—they showed a remarkable tenacity. Then there were the five executions, including the man suddenly gone crazy, who had roared and foamed. A nasty moment, that—for a second the whole current had stopped flowing. But his men had jumped in at once—he himself had acted quickly. The others were merely incorrigible stragglers and of no account.

And now, it was almost over and soon the homeland would be free. Free as it never had been—for, without the Accursed People, it would be unlike any other country on earth. They were gone, with their books and their music, their false, delusive science and their quick way of thinking. They were gone, all the people like Willi Schneider and his mother, who had spent so much time in talking and being friendly. They were gone, the willful people, who clung close together and yet so willfully supported the new and the untried. The men who haggled over pennies, and the others who gave—the sweater, the mimic, the philosopher, the discoverer—all were gone. Yes, and with them went their slaves' religion, the religion of the weak and the humble, the religion that fought so bitterly and yet exalted the prophet above the armed man.

One could be a whole man, with them gone, without their doubts and their mockery and their bitter, self-accusing laughter, their melancholy, deep as a well, and their endless aspiration for something that could not be touched with the hand. One could be solid and virile and untroubled, virile and huge as the old, thunderous gods. It was so that the Leader had spoken, so it must be true. And the countries who weakly received them would be themselves corrupted into warm unmanliness and mockery, into a desire for peace and a search for things not tangible. But the homeland would stand still and listen to the beat of its own heart—not even listen, but stand like a proud fierce animal, a perfect, living machine. To get children, to conquer others, to die gloriously in battle—that was the end of man. It had been a long time forgotten, but the Leader had remembered it. And, naturally, one could not do that completely with them in the land, for they had other ideas.

He thought of these things dutifully because it was right to think of them. They had been repeated and repeated in his ears till they had occupied his mind. But, meanwhile, he was very tired and the dust still rose. They were coming by clumps and groups,—now the last stragglers—they were no longer a solid, flowing current. The afternoon had turned hot—unseasonably hot. He didn't want any more brandy—the thought of it sickened his stomach. He wanted a glass of beer—iced beer, cold and dark, with foam on it—and a chance to unbutton his collar. He wanted to have the thing done and sit down and have Franz pull off his boots. If it were only a little cooler, a little quieter—if even these last would not wail so, now and then—if only the dust would not rise! He found himself humming, for comfort, a Christmas hymn—it brought a little, frail coolness to his mind.

> "Silent night, holy night,
> All is calm, all is bright...."

The old gods were virile and thunderous, but, down in the South, they would still deck the tree, in kindliness. Call it a custom—call it anything you like—it still came out of the heart. And it was a custom of the homeland—it could not be wrong. Oh, the beautiful, crisp snow of Christmas Day, the greetings between friends, the bright, lighted tree! Well, there'd be a Christmas to come. Perhaps he'd be married, by then—he had thought of it, often. If he were, they would have a tree—young couples were sentimental, in the South. A tree and a small manger beneath it, with the animals and the child. They carved the figures out of wood, in his country, with loving care—the thought of them was very peaceful and cool. In the old days, he had always given Willi Schneider part of his almond cake—one knew it was not Willi's festival but one was friendly, for all that. And that must be forgotten. He had had no right to give Willi part of his almond cake—it was the tree that mattered, the tree and the tiny candles, the smell of the fresh pine and the clear, frosty sweetness of the day. They would keep that, he and his wife, keep it with rejoicing, and Willi would not look in through the window, with his old face or his new face. He would not look in at all, ever any more. For now the homeland was released, after many years.

Now the dust was beginning to settle—the current in the road had dwindled to a straggling trickle. He was able to think, for the first time, of the land to which that trickle was going—a hungry land, the papers said, in spite of its boastful ways. The road led blankly into it, beyond the rise of ground—hard to tell what it was like. But they would be dispersed, not only here, but over many lands. Of course, the situation was not comparable—all the same, it must be a queer feeling. A queer feeling, yes, to start out anew, with nothing but the clothes on your back and what you could push in a handcart, if you had a handcart. For an instant the thought came, unbidden, "It must be a great people that can bear such things." But they were the Accursed People—the thought should not have come.

He sighed and turned back to his duty. It was really wonderful—even on the third day there was such order, such precision. It was something to be proud of—something to remember long. The Leader would speak of it, undoubtedly. The ones who came now were the very last stragglers, the weakest, but they were being moved along as promptly as if they were strong. The dust actually no longer rose in a cloud—it was settling, slowly but surely.

He did not quite remember when he had last eaten. It did not matter, for the sun was sinking fast, in a red warm glow. In a moment, in an hour, it would be done—he could rest and undo his collar, have some beer. There was nobody on the road now—nobody at all. He stood rigidly at his post—the picture of an officer, though somewhat dusty—but he knew that his eyes were closing. Nobody on the road—nobody for a whole five minutes... for eight... for ten.

He was roused by Franz's voice in his ear—he must have gone to sleep, standing up. He had heard of that happening to soldiers on the march—he felt rather proud that, now, it had happened to him. But there seemed to be a little trouble on the road he walked forward to it, stiffly, trying to clear his throat.

It was a commonplace grouping—he had seen dozens like it in the course of the three days—an older man, a young woman, and, of course, the child that she held. No doubt about them, either—the man's features were strongly marked, the woman had the liquid eyes. As for the child, that was merely a wrapped bundle. They should have started before—stupid people—the man looked strong enough. Their belongings were done up like all poor people's belongings.

He stood in front of them, now, erect and a soldier. "Well," he said. "Don't you know the orders? No livestock to be taken. Didn't they examine you, down the road?" ("And a pretty fool I'll look like, reporting one confiscated donkey to Headquarters," he thought, with irritation. "We've been able to manage, with the chickens, but this is really too much! What can they be thinking of at the inspection point? Oh, well, they're tired too, I suppose, but it's my responsibility.")

He put a rasp in his voice—he had to, they looked at him so stupidly. "Well?" he said. "Answer me! Don't you know an officer when you see one?"

"We have come a long way," said the man, in a low voice. "We heard there was danger to the child. So we are going. May we pass?" The voice was civil enough, but the eyes were dark and large, the face tired and worn. He was resting one hand on his staff, in a peasant gesture. The woman said nothing at all and one felt that she would say nothing. She sat on the back of the gray donkey and the child in her arms, too, was silent, though it moved.

The lieutenant tried to think rapidly. After all, these were the last. But the thoughts buzzed around his head and would not come out of his mouth. That was fatigue. It should be easy enough for a lieutenant to give an order.

He found himself saying, conversationally, "There are just the three of you?"

"That is all," said the man and looked at him with great simplicity. "But we heard there was danger to the child. So we could not stay any more. We could not stay at all."

"Indeed," said the lieutenant and then said again, "indeed,"

"Yes," said the man. "But we shall do well enough—we have been in exile before." He spoke patiently and yet with a certain authority. When the lieutenant did not answer, he laid his other hand on the rein of the gray donkey. It moved forward a step and with it, also, the child stirred and moved. The lieutenant, turning, saw the child's face now, and its hands, as it turned and moved its small hands to the glow of the sunset.

"If the lieutenant pleases—" said an eager voice, the voice of the Northern corporal.

"The lieutenant does not please," said the lieutenant. He nodded at the man. "You may proceed."

"But Lieutenant—" said the eager voice.

"Swine and dog," said the lieutenant, feeling something snap in his mind, "are we to hinder the Leader's plans because of one gray donkey? The order says—all out of the country by sunset. Let them go. You will report to me, Corporal, in the morning."

He turned on his heel and walked a straight line to the field hut, not looking back. When Franz, the orderly, came in a little later, he found him sitting in a chair.

"If the lieutenant would take some brandy—" he said, respectfully.

"The lieutenant has had enough brandy," said the lieutenant, in a hoarse, dusty voice. "Have my orders been obeyed?"

"Yes, Lieutenant."

"They are gone—the very last of them?"

"Yes, Lieutenant."

"They did not look back?"

"No, Lieutenant."

The lieutenant said nothing, for a while, and Franz busied himself with boots. After some time, he spoke.

"The lieutenant should try to sleep," he said. "We have carried out our orders. And now, they are gone."

"Yes," said the lieutenant, and, suddenly, he saw them again, the whole multitude, dispersed among every country—the ones who had walked his road, the ones at the points of embarkation. There were a great many of them, and that he had expected. But they were not dispersed as he had thought. They were not dispersed as he had thought, for, with each one went shame, like a visible burden. And the shame was not theirs, though they carried it—the shame belonged to the land that had driven them forth—his own land. He could see it growing and spreading like a black blot—the shame of his country spread over the whole earth.

"The lieutenant will have some brandy," he said. "Quickly, Franz."

When the brandy was brought, he stared at it for a moment, in the cup.

"Tell me, Franz," he said. "Did you know them well? Any of them? Before?"

"Oh yes, Lieutenant," said Franz, in his smooth, orderly's voice. "In the last war, I was billeted—well, the name of the town does not matter, but the woman was one of them. Of course that was before we knew about them," he said, respectfully. "That was more than twenty years ago. But she was very kind to me—I used to make toys for her children. I have often wondered what happened to her—she was very considerate and kind. Doubtless I was wrong, Lieutenant? But that was in another country."

"Yes, Franz," said the lieutenant. "There were children, you say?"

"Yes, Lieutenant."

"You saw the child today? The last one?"

"Yes, Lieutenant."

"Its hands had been hurt," said the lieutenant. "In the middle. Right through. I saw them. I wish I had not seen that. I wish I had not seen its hands."

Made in the USA
Lexington, KY
10 March 2017